The Artist
in the Pines

M. Reese Kennedy

**SUNKEN
GARDENS
PRESS**

www.sunkengardenspress.com

Cover Art: A Path in the Woods, Vincent Van Gogh, 1887. Van Gogh Museum,
Amsterdam

CONTENTS

PART ONE

1   A CHANCE ENCOUNTER   3
2   APPLES IN THE PEN   11
3   SKETCH ON A NAPKIN   16
4   ONE FOR THE MANTELPIECE   22
5   THE RUSTIC CABIN   29
6   DOMINION OF THE PINES   33
7   A SHINIER PURPOSE   39
8   PINE TREES BEFORE THE DUSK   43
9   THE HOMESTEADERS   51
10 GARDEN AT NOON WITH FIGURE   55
11 BLACK ICE   62
12 PONDSCAPE AT DAWN   67
13 THE CANDLELIT MARCH   72

PART TWO

14 THE GALLERY   79
15 NIGHTSPLITTING   84
16 THE SWORD IN THE STONE   88
17 LONG-LEGGED GUESTS   94
18 THE CAROTENE CAT   99
19 A RUDE INTERRUPTION   105
20 APPLE TREES ON A SUMMER AFTERNOON   110
21 UP ON THE PLANKS   117
22 THE GOLDEN SPIKE   122
23 AN UNEXPECTED SWIM   130
24 A NIGHT AT THE MOVIES   137
25 THE BLUEBERRY FARM   145
26 THE VITRUVIAN MAN   151
27 PORTRAIT OF A DUCK   155
28 THE CHANGING OF THE SEASONS   161
29 AN EARTHY SLEEP   165
30 AFTERWORD   169

PART ONE

Chapter 1

A CHANCE ENCOUNTER

He stepped into view on a day so warm that the pines oozed resin and the forest was thick with its vapors. We'd just entered that dreamy place known as the afternoon nap, my four-year-old a marionette snipped from his strings, crumpled on the daybed in the shade of the porch roof. I was settled on the adjoining deck, soaking up my sliver of the sun in an Adirondack chair, a tall glass of lemonade perspiring on one of its arms. From that seat, I had a commanding view of the crumbly asphalt road, as it appeared from the woods a quarter mile to the east, and as it bent by the beaver pond in its approach to our cabin. The stranger seemed to stride right out of the trees, a mirage walker shimmering in the heat.

Even at distance I could see he moved with a smooth and effortless gait. It spoke of a certain proficiency, as if he were accustomed to a good deal of walking. His hat was full-brimmed, like something from an old western, and he displayed it amply with the many tilts and turns of his head. He was scanning – the trees, the pond, the sky – searching, like a birdwatcher for a hawk owl, or a zealot for a revelation. He glided along as if by some sixth sense, looking everywhere but straight ahead while never breaking stride or veering in the slightest. I could see now that the hat was more like something an old farmer might have worn, made of straw, soft and a little droopy along the brim. That made him only slightly less out of place here. He wasn't in cowboy country or in farmland. He was deep in the northern pine forest.

As he rounded the bend he stopped perfectly still, staring out toward the pond and the beaver lodge. That lodge was the obvious focal point for anyone walking this road. Even the most indifferent wanderer could see the artistry in that dome of gnawed sticks and packed mud, crudely majestic in its jut from the water. And this wanderer was far from indifferent. He didn't look so much as he studied, processing views as if committing them to memory. He turned from the pond straight to me – the shift was abrupt and instinctive, almost theatrical, as if I'd shouted out to him. I couldn't see his eyes, but I could feel that stare boring in. He held it there, longer than common decency would allow, long enough that I nearly stood to face it. But he broke it off and set to his stride as before.

His clothes were curiously lacking in both color and shape. On his back he carried what might be called a rucksack, an earthy-looking bag, something I imagined woodfolk had once used to forage. I could see this man, dressed just as he was, gathering nuts or digging for truffles in some older, darker forest – and dropping them, with gnarled and blackened fingers, into just such a bag. He reached the culvert, where the stream passed under the road, crossed it, and began the gentle ascent along the line of our land. The fieldstone wall was no taller than my knee, but it sat on a small bank and so concealed all but his head and shoulders. Even those slipped in and out of view as he began to pass the great pines that dwarfed the road.

Over one shoulder he'd slung a leather quiver, large enough to carry a couple dozen sturdy arrows from an earlier age. In their place it held some lengths of wood and several long papery rolls tied with ribbon or string. The pace of his walk was more apparent as he drew near and began to flash past the massive trunks of pine. But, as if on some silent command, he stopped short. He fingered the stubble of his reddish beard. His low-set position behind the wall, perfectly framed by two of the trees, suggested a portrait of a man in a trench. He looked back where he'd been, and then again at the cabin and at me.

"Might I pause here to make a sketch?" he asked.

His accent was heavily European, but he spoke slowly enough for me to understand. Or so I thought.

"Fine by me," I answered.

He said nothing more, but to my great surprise he walked up our driveway, past the little front patch of our shadowed lawn, past the single enormous pine at the corner of the house, and right up our front stairs. I stood to face him, but, with a quick nod to me, and a glance at my sleeping son, he walked right by, straight to the railing at the edge of the deck. There, with his back to me, and his hands on his hips, he settled in for a long look at the pond. Or was it the pines that had his attention? The afternoon was dead still at that moment, as if in concert with the stranger's motionless stance at the rail. I could see now that his quiver held rolls of canvas, each tied in strips of leather, and a baguette wrapped in baker's paper.

A hint of a breeze stirred the trees, and with that the trance was ended. The man peeled off his bundles and knelt to remove some lengths of wood. These he pieced together with a practiced air, threading bolts and twirling wing nuts with the nimble fingers of an elf. Before I could manage a guess, he'd assembled a good-sized easel, larger than anything I'd imagined he might conjure from what he'd carried. Neither of us had said a word since he'd come onto the deck. I'd been too astonished at first, and now I was just curious to see how far this would go. He snapped together a clever frame and leaned it against the porch rail. He unrolled a canvas and began tacking it to the stretching frame with a small ball-peen hammer. I'd have needed a workbench, clamps, and twenty minutes – but he knocked it off in just a minute or two, perched on one knee, setting it perfectly taut on all four edges. He swapped the hammer for a pencil, stood to place the canvas, and, without the slightest hesitation, he began to sketch, in short, decisive strokes. As if by the labor of unseen stagehands, my private sanctuary, my hand-built wilderness sundeck, had become something entirely different – a woodshop, a studio, a platform for a roaming mime.

Still not a word was spoken. His sketching was brisk, almost frenzied, as if he were racing to a deadline. He paused only to shoot me an imperious and proprietary look, suggesting, it seemed, that I leave him alone at his workplace. I wasn't going to leave my own deck – that much was certain. On the contrary, I had an impulse to jump up and shove him back down the stairs. But something quieted within me, urged me to let it play out. I took a breath and settled back into my chair. I feigned disinterest, as if this sort of thing happened every day. I looked back down the road, sipped at my lemonade. I wondered at his clothes – they had the beginnings of the greasy sheen you'd see on a drifter, but I was more struck by their unusual styling, the collarless button-down shirt, the shapeless brown trousers, and the shoes, a type I hadn't seen before, ankle-high with only three eyelets and well-worn brown uppers, thick like saddle leather.

"Are you settling in for a stretch?" I asked, unable to resist the hint of sarcasm.

"I sketch until I am ready for paint," he answered softly.

Had he thought I'd said "sketch"? I let it go for the moment. I looked out over the pond and listened to his pencil scraping over the canvas, knowing now that this was just a preamble to a longer project. What kind of person would take such liberties? My quiet time was a precious commodity, the constant secret quest of every single parent. My curiosity was yielding once more to irritation, to the point where I stood again, this time to end it, to direct the strange-mannered intruder off my porch. But when he turned to me, his look was so disarming – not quite friendly, but somehow kindred – and he showed such obvious pain to be torn from his work, that for a moment I felt bad for him. I heard myself say instead:

"You want a glass of lemonade?"

This was far more surprising to me, apparently, than to him. He answered matter-of-factly:

"Yes, just a modicum, very good, thank you."

I stared at him for a moment. What kind of person says modicum? With an odd little bob – a slight, stiff bending at the waist – was it really a bow? – he turned back to the canvas. I took a look before heading to the kitchen. It was the pines he'd been after, and I could see at once that he had some skill with the pencil.

"They are wonderful trees," he said, as I came back with his glass. "How do you call them?"

"White pines. I'm Jason, by the way. This is my house." The pronouncement was absurd enough to actually embarrass me. I needed to have more conversations with adults – I knew that – but I didn't need to go kowtowing to the first hobo who wandered by. And it was irritating introducing myself to one who wouldn't bother introducing himself back. He gulped half the glass and produced a grotty handkerchief to wipe his lips and red whiskers. He thanked me for the drink – he did have the decency for that – and something through his accent struck me as educated, perhaps even aristocratic, in contrast to his slovenly appearance and erratic manner. I took another look at the canvas. What I saw in that instant, just a few pencil strokes after I'd glimpsed it the first time, put me strangely off my mark. I offered my hand but felt a tinge of regret as he shifted the handkerchief to take it.

His age was unclear, anywhere from thirty to fifty, though I pegged him at the lower end of that scale. His eyes were watery pools of blue, observant and possibly intelligent, if a bit droopy in the lower lids. There was something unusual about the way he looked at things. I could almost see the shutter action of his pupils as he turned his focus on me through the glare of the sun. He was naturally fair-skinned, but no stranger to the outdoors. His hand was freckled, with tightly trimmed nails, unremarkable in all respects until he lifted the pencil and resumed his flurry at the canvas. The sketch was taking shape at a freakish rate, like a silent artist-at-work film clip run at triple speed. He threw me another resentful look, clearly offended by my staring over his shoulder. This time I nearly laughed out loud. But fair enough, I thought. I retreated to my seat, to the view I'd seen from that deck at all hours of the day, in every season, in all imaginable weather – but never, apparently, quite like he had. I sipped my lemonade and looked out toward the pond, reframing the familiar trees as I'd just seen them on the canvas.

Unlike some pines that grow in an almost uniformly conical fashion, each white pine has a character of its own. The branches are both spare and sporadic, unevenly spaced, but they spread in something approaching a true horizontal, often running twenty feet or more before the first clusters of their long and wispy needles. The soft wood of white pines is particularly susceptible to heavy winds – scarring from the occasional lost limb gives them an even more jagged and animated appearance. They creaked now in the gathering breeze, as they often did if you stopped to listen, like mainmasts on the great wooden-hulled ships of centuries past. One squirrel chased another, circling up a tree in a perfect barber pole pattern. A pair of bluejays posed shamelessly. It was all suddenly and absurdly idyllic. The sun was warming, tranquilizing. The scratching of the pencil had a bit of a hypnotic effect. And, unlikely as it seemed with this stranger on my deck, I drifted off, seeming to leave my body in the chair and to float in some dreamy stand of mossy old-growth.

After some time, and as if from some great distance, I heard him announce that his sketching was complete. "The light was more favorable an hour ago," he said, consulting an ancient-looking pocket watch.

"I will need to paint at that time tomorrow. Also, I will see it in the early morning. May I to use your commode?"

I shouldn't have slept, I thought, instantly awake and checking for Blake. He was still asleep on the daybed. Commode? Who says commode? And did he say tomorrow? For the third time, I grunted out of my chair. I took another look at the canvas – the sketch was remarkable – just as I realized that my leg was fast asleep. Trying not to show a limp, my leg screaming and that sketch flashing in alternate frames through my mind, I led him along the familiar planks of the deck and across the covered porch. His gaze settled again on Blake.

"The child sleeps beautifully," he said.

As we turned to the door, he reached out to touch the log wall, as if to rule out a faux exterior. Our cabin was the real thing, built of whole logs, ten inches in diameter, milled flat on two sides to stack cleanly, spiked at intervals, interlocking in the corners. Whether this made an impression, I couldn't say – he was leaning on the wall only to remove his shoes. His socks were the color of parched earth. I preferred him in shoes but said nothing.

Two simple rooms flanked a central pine staircase to make up the first floor. I led him through the kitchen to the right. His eyes moved to the huge overhead crossbeam, to the stress cracks that always seemed ominous to visitors, and to the pots and pans dangling from eyehooks over a butcher-block table eighteen inches thick. As I'd seen on the road, he seemed to have an ability to navigate while looking anywhere but ahead – now in these tight quarters it was almost eerie, a kind of human echolocation.

When he came out of the bathroom he circled back the other way, through the living room, where New England style furniture gathered around a black cast-iron woodstove. He seemed to take in the whole room at once. The logs, weathered tan on the outside, were stained a golden brown in here. There were wide floorboards of knotty pine, exposed beams bearing second-story floorboards of the same knotty cut, a brick chimney, sunny six-over-six windows — and a little bed in the corner, with a dinosaur quilt and a sleeping cat.

"If you would be so kind, I would like to make camp."

"OK," I said, intoning this more as a question than an answer. He didn't seem to catch the distinction. He was already out the door.

Chapter 2

APPLES IN THE PEN

It was Blake, as usual, who ushered in the morning. He padded up the stairs and into my room at the normal hour, just before six. His bare feet moved quickly from the hardwood to the area rug, and he bounded up into my bed. I threw an arm around him, warmed his feet, tried to snuggle him back to sleep. But as much as I wished for it, there was no more rest in the boy. He was full of morning mischief, pretending to sleep, then squirming and giggling while I clamped him in place. When at last I let him go, he slung his legs over the side and dropped to the floor. I stood and stretched, then remembered the artist. I looked through the window for his simple tent, really just a piece of old-time army-grade canvas, faded into greenish grays and yellowish browns as I'd seen it draped and staked at sunset. But now the lawn sat empty, unoccupied. If not for the telling patches in the dew, I'd have thought I'd dreamed the whole thing up.

"Looks like our visitor has moved on," I said, turning from the window and reaching for a shirt. I hadn't known whether to admire him as a gifted and dedicated pilgrim of the arts, or to dismiss him as some lunatic toting canvases and baguettes in a quiver. I now wrote him off as the latter and followed Blake down the steps.

We began the morning ritual as we'd been doing for the last few weeks. I held him in the crook of my arm, and he grasped a heavy wooden spoon to bash the timpani of pots and pans dangling from the kitchen beam. It was something he'd done as a much younger child and had come back to of late. He had a bit of rooster in him – I figured that was the best way to explain it. This would have been a great way to roust the stranger, I thought through the din, unable to shake the feeling that he'd somehow had the better of us. The cookware clamor didn't bother me much – my head pounded most mornings, with or without it. Blake was in full mettle, left arm clasped around my neck, head up in the full throes of concentration, right arm banging away. All the pots in his reach were in motion, swinging on their eyehooks, more difficult now to strike dead center. It made for an irregular beat, but the tones were not altogether discordant, more like wind chimes from some large-featured nether world. I read his eyes, taking a step or two along the line of the beam to make the bigger pans available as soon as he looked for them. We always saved the cast iron fryer for last. It hung at the end of the row and put out the most impressive gongs. A familiar fatigue began to creep into my right bicep. Blake was getting heavier by the month, and it was awkward leaning out over the butcher-block.

Children are a resilient bunch, I thought. Like the pines, they're susceptible to scarring, but they seem to tar over their wounds and keep on to the real work of growing up, in their assigned time, right on schedule. In a way, he'd hardly known his mother. And yet to that point she'd been his entire life, his food, his shelter, his warmth, his laughter. But the way of the world had prevailed, the planet, as always, spinning us into one new morning and then another, awakening a host of new adventures at each turn. He'd had no choice but to throw himself back in. So much encountered, so much learned, he'd packed the days around her like old blankets in an attic closet, and he'd kept moving. My biceps strained to failure as the percussion of pots and pans reached its crescendo. I lowered him to the floor, straightened back up, and there, through the window, was a walker, approaching briskly from the west.

"Ah, here he is again," I said. I gripped Blake's hand, and we headed to the door. Blake is fond of visitors, I thought. As the screen door shut behind us, the artist was just reaching the porch steps. I expected a brief conversation on the threshold, but he walked right on by, just as he'd done the day before, with the same wordless nod. He headed straight for the easel, which I now saw he'd tucked against the covered wall, near his neatly folded tent.

"The morning light is very good," he said.

He set the easel on the same patch of deck as before and knelt again at his rucksack. This time he withdrew a smock, which he pulled quickly over his head, and two bundles wrapped in cloth. One held a well-used wooden palette, the other a host of brushes, paint tubes and solvent jars. He worked the tubes with practiced, efficient movements – capping and uncapping, squeezing neat little mounds of oil paint onto the palette, replacing everything just so.

"Do I need to spread a tarp?" I asked, motioning with a sweep of my hand at the deck floor, spotless but for a few bird drops since the last scrubbing. Blake aped my movements, pointing with his wooden spoon.

The artist poked his thumb through the hole in the palette and swept it into the crook of his arm. His fingers cupped a riot of unmatched brushes, more than half a dozen, into a gap cut at the palette's edge. "No, no, you needn't worry with spills," he said. This wasn't all that convincing, especially in view of the horrible stains covering his smock. I reached for Blake's free hand and took him inside for breakfast.

Through our kitchen window, a white coat of dew still cloaked the Parenteaus' field, out beyond our shared driveway and the fieldstone wall that ran just beyond it. That wall was of the same crude build as the one along the road, the kind that seemed to run everywhere in that part of the country, even through woods so deep you'd think they'd never been farmed. On the far side of the field, where the land began to fall off, apple trees marched in full leaf toward the little pigpen, and beyond it to the lake.

"Will the man draw the big fat pigs?" Blake asked.

"He's a painter, Blake. I think he's just going to paint the trees."

"I'll check," he said, still chewing as he crashed back out the screen door. I took a quick gulp and followed him out. We both stopped at the same moment – a cardinal flittered past, curled, and settled in a bush. In a few months that bush would be as red as the bird. For now the summer morning was brilliant on the deck. Even better, the floor-boards on the deck were still unsmudged. I decided a mug of coffee would serve as a reward for the tidy artist and went back in for it. As I was pouring, Blake's little voice filtered through the screens:

"What's your name?"

There was a long pause before the response.

"Please, you can call me Willem."

"Mister Willem," I hollered out from the kitchen.

"Mister Willem," Blake had to stop and take a breath, "Do you want to see the big fat pigs?"

Another long pause preceded his answer.

"I seem to be occupied at present. But perhaps later in the morning. And thank you, Master…" He ended on a questioning note and another bow, this one unmistakable, full and formal, as he turned to me for his cup. I judged that he appreciated it, based on a couple of wolfish swallows.

"Blake. The boy's name is Blake. If you don't mind, I'll let him sit and watch you while I clean up. Then I'll take him for a walk and leave you to your work." He seemed harmless enough, I thought.

We didn't have a dishwasher, and I didn't see much use for one. I'd always been happy enough with a sink full of suds and a wooden strainer racked for drying. A familiar task, a raft of tiny logistical decisions bobbing in a sea of reflections — there was an element of refuge in it. Blake would often sit near me on the floor, pulling cans from the cupboard and piling them like toy blocks in wobbly stacks, always the broad-based tuna at the bottom. But at the moment there was no such construction — he was still chattering on the deck, though I couldn't quite catch the conversation. With only a dish or two to go, I resolved to relieve the artist. But just then the two of them appeared through the window. Blake was leading him up the driveway, porcine introductions in the offing. The pigs knew Blake well enough, by his green-and-blue striped shirt if nothing else. He'd worn that shirt, along with his black duck-billed cap, every day for the last two months. I'd let him pick his own clothes from the first day he'd shown any inclination, and if he wanted that shirt I wasn't going to bully him on the point. It was a small concession to throw it in a quick wash and have it laid out fresh for him in the morning.

I took my time — racked the last dish, wiped down the table, hung the towel — then headed out the back door to join them. Blake was standing on the first rail of the pen. He tossed in an apple, and as he turned to climb down for another I was there to hand him two more. I lifted him onto the second rail and held him there, where his sight line was clean and he could toss apples comfortably over the top. The pigs, three healthy adolescents, put on a show, as they always did. They quick-stepped over, snorting enthusiastically, and nuzzled the apples well into the mud before chomping into the bright white cores. The first three apples were gone. Before Blake could scramble down, the artist was there to hand him another.

Chapter 3

SKETCH ON A NAPKIN

I hardly ever locked the doors in our piece of the forest. With a drifter on the deck I suppose I should have. And the thought did cross my mind. But when Blake and I headed out for our walk, I left the house wide open. I'd pocketed the truck keys, and the tools were in the lock-box. I figured there wasn't much else he was going to haul out on foot – worst case a six-pack and a couple pair of socks. Odd as he was, I didn't read him as a thief, and I was feeling pretty indifferent that morning anyway. So I told him to help himself to a glass of water, or to the bathroom, or "commode", as he needed. Without abandoning his naturally solemn air, he showed an appreciation so heartfelt, mostly with a series of bows – to me, to Blake, and back to me – that I wondered whether to be happy right with him or to regret my decision all the more.

Blake made it halfway around the lake on his own that morning, a good long walk at his age. He liked to look at the water – it seemed to have a mesmerizing effect on even a four-year-old. After a while, when the lake disappeared behind the trees, he became more active, picking up sticks, kicking mushrooms, blowing dandelions into clouds of white sparkles. We lingered at the head of the old logging trail, where he poked a stick at a dead and quickly drying snake. "Not many cars on this road," I said. "He must have picked a bad time to crawl across. Or a bad place for sunbathing."

Splattered roadkill – just another in the millions of daily casualties in a harsh and random domain. Here was Blake, contemplating the dead creature and moving on, and here was I, bringing him up in just such a world. Somehow the new reality hadn't quite crushed either of us. Blake climbed a stone wall, and I steadied him with one hand while he leaned and lurched along the top of it. After ten or fifteen steps he'd worked enough. He turned to face me and took my other hand. I floated him down. We set back into the walk, and he picked up another stick to poke at things along the way.

When we started up the incline that marked the far side of the lake, he tired for good and indicated the move onto my shoulders. I lifted him up over my head and settled him onto his familiar perch. He spent the rest of the walk there, his tiny hands pressed to my forehead, my own hands clasping his little shoes, his chin resting sporadically on the crown of my head. We came around the final bend, where the road leaves the lake and returns by the beaver pond. Blake spotted the artist, still at his easel. He wiggled off my shoulders and ran from the crumbling edge of the road, across the carpet of needles under the pines, past the edge of the knee wall, and diagonally across the yard. I joined him a minute later on the deck, where he stood at the artist's hip, motionless and staring.

With a strip of blacktop on one side and cleared land on the other, the pines along the road had enjoyed very little competition over many decades. They'd flourished theatrically as a result. I figured them to be a hundred twenty-five feet tall, with diameters approaching four feet. I was rather proud of them, though I certainly couldn't take any credit. I was a spectator only, a passer-through, a resident admirer. The artist, more transient here than I, seemed less impressed with their scale than their texture. His pines were slightly compressed, but amplified in their gnarliness and in the ridges and colors of their bark, which he'd shown in a fantastical rough-hewn shimmer of purples and blues. The effect was dreamy, but coarse enough to bloody your knuckles. The wind-sheared limbs were great open wounds, borne stoically, testaments to the stout character of the pines. At their base, simple golden strokes made blades of long midsummer grass, bowed as if in mourning. I could feel its wispiness as if it were brushing my pant legs.

Blake spoke first. "Those are good trees, Mister Willem. Why did you make them purple?" It was a fair question. Were those colors in the bark as fanciful as they seemed?

I'd been caught up in the painting, but now I was watching the artist himself. He was slow to answer, either irritated at our intrusion or working himself out of whatever trance he happened to work in. I noticed a clay jug at his feet, corked.

"Look closely in the early morning, Master Blake," he said at last. "See what the light shows you. Maybe you will see purple then too."

Better late than never, I thought. I considered his answer, then asked a question of my own: "How do you remember the early morning colors when you're still painting at noon? Don't the colors keep changing with the sun?"

Again the artist was silent. I began to think he wasn't going to answer. Was he speaking only to children? But in time he answered this too:

"As the day progresses, so its colors do also. A painting takes a full day for me, sometimes two, but it must be made as if in a single moment. So I make the colors on my palette at the beginning, colors from the light I feel is best, and I work with that palette to the finish. In that way it is early morning all day."

OK, I thought, maybe it's a language thing, or maybe he just thinks before he speaks, which isn't necessarily a bad thing. Either way, I was relieved at his civility, however painfully extracted.

"That may be true," I said. "But even if it's morning all day, there has to be a lunchtime. I would put it right about now."

Any cleverness in the remark – and granted, there was very little – eluded both members of my audience. And not for the last time, I imagined. But offering lunch was the only humane thing to do. The artist had been on our periphery since mid-afternoon the day before, and to my knowledge he hadn't eaten anything more than a few chunks of his baguette. He was sturdily enough built, broad enough in the shoulders, but a hollow in his cheeks suggested a touch of deprivation, the hunger of the stray.

It was no trouble to include him. Blake and I were well drilled in sandwich production and welcomed the challenge of the third party. I set a chair at the kitchen table. Blake climbed to a standing position and laid out six slices of bread. I put the fixings on the bottom slices, while Blake, with a great grimace on his face and his little elbows spread wide, set to open the jar of mayonnaise. After a moment, the lid popped free. He exhaled dramatically and looked to me for comment. "Strong like moose!" I said. He grinned, and I grinned back. This tripped me up, and for a moment I was somewhere else – but I reined myself in and spread the mayonnaise. He flipped the tops, closing out the three sandwiches in turn. I moved them onto plates, and we carried them, with napkins and drinks, onto the deck.

I pulled over a couple of Adirondacks and motioned for the artist to join us. Yesterday's trip to the pigpen notwithstanding, my early impression was that he had to be more or less starving to be lured from the easel. He seemed conflicted – fidgety and ill at ease – as he lowered himself into his chair. He had his water jug in one hand, but when he saw we'd already set him a drink he seemed confused for a moment. He was just setting the jug on the deck when Blake let fly a question. "Mister Willem, why is your board so messy?"

I'd wondered the same thing; his palette was as hopeless as his smock, chaotic with colors smudged and smeared beyond recognition, a far cry from the neat piles of unspoiled color we'd seen squeezed from the tubes that morning. I might not have asked that question first, or as abruptly as Blake, before our visitor had even settled into his sandwich. But, as it happened, he was perfectly willing to answer any question of that sort. To the extent that he wasn't gorging himself – I got up after a few minutes to make another sandwich to split between us – he was fully conversational in his art, and careful to include Blake at every turn. But with any question that probed at his person – Where did he come from? Where was he headed? Did he have a family? – his accent seemed to thicken, and he'd become nearly unintelligible. Or he'd wander with his words, coloring and framing his speech until he'd answered an entirely different question. Before too long even Blake seemed to notice – the slightest prying made for an awkward and unsatisfactory exchange.

But in quiet company, or with a backdrop of Blake's simple chatter, the artist would come to life, and our little party with him. He had a wonder for the natural world that was a perfect fit for a spell on our deck. He asked about the beaver lodge, and I explained the animal's aptitude for engineering and its overall strategy with the dam and the lodge. He seemed to have some familiarity with the beaver, but it was vaguely recalled, as if from another life – he also heard these things like a child, as if for the first time. Helping myself to his pencil, I sketched a vertical section of the lodge on my paper napkin. I illustrated the iceberg effect, only the top part of the lodge showing above the water line. Below it, I showed the underwater entrance, the drying chamber, the cozy living quarters. The artist seemed intrigued. He handed me another napkin, his own, slightly soiled but not crumpled, and had me draw the animal itself. At Blake's insistence, I put special emphasis on its big tree-cutting teeth and its paddle-flat tail. I explained that it used its tail like a bicycle kickstand when it stood to chew trees, and to slap the water when it felt threatened. The artist seemed to reflect on this as he studied my sketch. After a moment he unfolded the napkin and motioned for his pencil. I handed it over, and he too began to draw. It was no more than doodling for him, but in a short minute my ridiculous little beaver found itself in a perfect little habitat – a stand of saplings, two of them gnawed like the point of the pencil, and water reeds, and a pond revealed only by their rippled reflections.

"That's really good, Mister Willem," said Blake. For a four-year-old especially, it was a massive understatement. Normally, we use cotton napkins – I hate running through paper, and, as mentioned, I do a load of laundry every day anyway. But for some reason I'd set the plain paper napkins for this meal, and now I had a powerful urge to snag his right back. I resisted for a moment – it had stains from his lunch for god's sake. But I grabbed it in spite of myself and tucked it away, taking pains not to crumble or further crease it. I slipped him a new one for the rest of his meal. Neither he nor Blake seemed to notice the exchange.

He was very much in his element eating outdoors. He'd take a bite, set his sandwich carefully back on the plate, then look up into the sky, watching the clouds and the movements of the trees as he chewed. He was straight and somewhat formal in his posture – that seemed in his nature. But his eyes were glowing with life, and his hands seemed at peace, folded restfully in his lap. As we finished our sandwiches a sparrow danced on the porch rail, and Blake and I, and then the artist, tossed him our crumbs. With the last of them, the bird was off. The artist thanked us for the lunch and returned to his easel.

Chapter 4

ONE FOR THE MANTELPIECE

Blake and I grabbed our ballgloves and headed out. We wandered across the driveway and through the cut in the fieldstone wall, meandering as four-year-olds do. We dared in turns to touch the stones – the afternoon sun had baked them hot, and Blake howled and danced and pretended he'd burned his hand off. We eventually did take the field, where we made a few tosses, then took a break to watch some particularly white and puffy clouds pass over the tree-line. The screen door slammed, and we knew the Parenteau boys had sniffed out the game. They'd join right in – we'd be disappointed if they didn't. Our playing in their field, rather than our own, was a kind of invitation, though they were just as likely to join in at our place. The door slammed again. The Parenteau boys never approached together, but in a staggered formation, as if they wanted nothing to do with each other. Koby led the parade. He was short and athletic, with an oversized head and a smile that was strangely ironic, at least for a boy of his age. Jamie, already as tall as his older brother, but far more delicate, would follow. He was the gentlest and warmest of the three, though he always seemed to be looking off somewhere. The screen door slammed for a third time, and Kevin was the last to appear. A caricature of a boy, with bruised shins, missing teeth, and a crewcut, Kevin was the family jester, something semi-solid forever poking from his nose.

We played a lot of pickle in those days. Blake was too young to make much use of his glove – he'd hold it in front of him and I'd need to toss the ball right in – but Koby and Jamie could catch and throw pretty well. I took one bag, and those two would rotate on the other. But what all the boys really wanted to do was run, Blake and two of the Parenteaus dancing between the bases, drawing the throw, feinting, waiting, then sprinting and sliding in the grass, squirming to avoid the tag. They loved the occasional overthrow, hollering and taking two or three bases at a time while the beleaguered gloveman, usually me, chased the errant toss.

Karl Parenteau wasn't one to play with his kids. He was a tradesman, not a game-player. He was balding and thickly moustached, slight of build, with thin legs that rarely saw the sun. His eyes would sometimes sparkle with life and humor, but they were most often turned to a task. Perhaps it was just his nature, but I had the impression that his relentless industry was a form of homage to his wife, the lady of the house. Betty was his height, or just taller, with nice skin and teeth, an overlarge head on tiny shoulders, and a slight lisp. She hailed from Pinewoods, just as Karl did – they'd been high school sweethearts – and I'm not sure she'd ever ventured far from home. But she carried a certain worldly confidence about her, an air of slightly superior stock. They both considered her the smarter one, and the feeling was she might well have done better. He would make it up by working all the harder to give her the lifestyle she warranted. He headed out early five mornings a week as an air conditioning mechanic. He'd moonlight on weekends. And when he wasn't on the clock he'd be on assignment around the premises, cracking at a catalog of odd jobs. "The Honeydew List," they called it, without a hint of embarrassment. He was fond of his boys and enjoyed watching them for a time. But it was never long before one of those projects would steal him away.

We had an unspoken agreement, Karl and I, in our enclave of two lots carved out of the forest. He kept his field impeccably mowed. He put in a nice basket at the end of the driveway. He kept the pigs, plowed our shared drive, advised me on my carpentry, helped me from time to time with my plumbing. I put in the time, taught his boys how to field, how to throw, how to shoot a proper jumpshot. I made them lunch, tossed them frisbees, let them hang around the house for hours on end. And in turn, Blake had a family at his disposal, a place to stay when I was away, and a bundle of boys to chum around with, far gentler than any older brothers could ever have been. At the pickle game's end the sweaty, grass-stained Parenteau boys began to trail us home, as they always did. But this day was a little different.

"Boys, you'll have to head on home today," I said. "We have an artist at the house, and he won't want to be disturbed." They seemed surprised, but complied with little comment, more intrigued by the news than disappointed at having their visiting hours cut.

The artist was still laboring at his station on the deck. But for the lunch break he'd been at it steadily, all the long day. Still, he worked at a frenetic pace. The painting seemed nearly complete. Green needles had appeared on the pines, interspersed and overlaid with the rippling purple bark. They seemed alive, quivering, more animal than plant. They all but prickled at the touch. He'd picked up on the obvious fact that panoramic skies aren't a signature experience in a forest of giant pines. His sky was a suitably small patch on the painting, but astonishing in its texture. I couldn't tell at first if the effect was from different colors of paint or different thicknesses of paint – grooves carved like elevations in a raised-relief map – but that sky was thick enough to swim in. I stepped back. I stepped forward. I couldn't stop looking. And neither could the Parenteau boys, apparently. They'd snuck up onto the porch, and, once discovered, scrambled off with impish grins. When I turned back the artist was standing between me and the canvas, glaring and breathing heavily.

"Come on Blake, let's go inside," I said, a bit sheepishly, though I might have sent the surly bastard packing if the painting hadn't been coming along so well.

It was several hours later, with the sun well below the tree line, when he brought it in to dry. The chicken was slow-cooking on the grill, and Blake was in the driveway, pedaling his Big-Wheel tricycle while the Parenteau boys whizzed up and down on their bikes, laying scratch and spraying pebbles. I was making the salad when I noticed the artist holding the painting with both hands, just outside the screen door. I wasn't sure how long he'd been standing there. He hadn't spoken, hadn't asked for help, but waited there with the quiet resolve of a well-mannered dog. I half-expected him to scratch a paw at the screen. When I did open the door, he sidled in, and the cat, as cats do, picked just that moment to dart outside, through our two sets of legs. This startled him, but he kept his grip and reset his stride. I noticed he was in stocking feet – once again he'd left his shoes at the door. He moved straight to the mantelpiece and set the painting there. That was the best place for it. There weren't any other obvious drying spots in the house, as he must have determined earlier. But the position had a certain connotation to it, a certain air of permanence. And the painting took on a different, more accomplished feel in the muted indoor light. I threw the artist a look of comical satisfaction, as if to say, "Good luck getting that back." He gave me an odd look – almost pained – and crashed back out the door.

And then I really took a look. I'd seen it in its parts, in its progression, but now, seeing the completed whole, my reaction was one of utter bewilderment. And rather than abating over the next few minutes, that feeling escalated, to disorientation, and then to something like shock. I was willing to concede good, even very good – had I been in the woods too long? – but this was fantastic, extraordinary, singular, like nothing I'd ever seen. His technique seemed proficient enough, but it wasn't craftsmanship that set it apart. This was graphic narration of a fantastical sort, a portal to another world, a secret marriage of the commonplace and the enchanted. The effect was stunning – I realized that I hadn't moved for a couple minutes now – without even considering the source, the strange and solitary drifter who'd wandered into our forest to paint. He'd done it in a single day, right before our eyes. When I'd cleared my head enough to reflect, the painting struck me on another level, as a stunning piece of optimism from such a taciturn and seemingly damaged man. It would take me weeks to digest it. To tell the truth, I'm still digesting it now.

Much as I wanted to, I couldn't stand in front of that painting any longer. Dinner always seemed to slip late enough when the summer evenings stretched so long. With all the outdoor air, the chorus of the frogs, the sounds of bicycles and basketballs and screen doors slamming, sometimes Blake would be too riled up to eat if I didn't slip his bath in beforehand. We were both old hands at bathtub protocol, the water temperature just right, bubbles piled like snow to his shoulders. I wielded the washcloth, and he reacted by rote, lifting his arms and shutting his eyes. When we'd finished the scrubbing he played with his bath toys while I sat abstracted on the three-legged wooden stool. It was a way we had of unwinding together.

The giant bath sponge was still there on the shelf. Annie and I had used it when Blake was a baby. It was six inches thick with a body imprint carved out on one side, like a little homicide victim drawn in chalk. Blake had fit perfectly into that hollow, secured at the base of the tub and well presented for soaping. This had solved my baby bath phobia, my fear of the slimy infant slipping out of my grip, cracking his head and sliding under the water. Annie, of course, had no such fears, but she did think Blake was cute nestled into that sponge. I thought about her now, as I always did, until the bubbles had gone flat and the water cool.

Blake was clean and quiet, settled in pajamas in one corner of the big easy chair. The washing machine whirred quietly from the basement, readying his striped shirt for another day. He was flipping through one of his books, but I noticed he was mostly just staring at the new painting on our mantel. I was headed out to pull the chicken, but I stopped for a moment to join him, allowing myself another look. I gawked from directly in front, then from the couch, the reading chair, from every point in the room. I walked up close. It was all I could do not to touch it directly, to press a thumbnail into the lingering wetness in the grooves and globs of paint. The thing had a bit of a hologram effect – how could such a hodgepodge up close look so divine a foot or two back? I mentioned this to Blake, but he seemed somehow to have already grasped the point.

I was no great connoisseur of the arts, but I wasn't ignorant either. I had a completely worthless master's degree to prove that. It struck me, the more I looked at it, that I'd been on the mark just earlier, that the painting really was something ingenious, an impression so mastered and stylistic and original that it was both an exact rendering of its subject matter and nothing at all like it. An improvement on the unimprovable, it was nature made timeless, ungrounded, alive and breathing. There on the mantel it was a divine coat of arms, dignifying the land and our small claim on it like nothing else I could imagine.

I pulled myself outside to tend the chicken. As I opened the grill, I couldn't help but look again, through the window. Even from a distance, from there on the deck, unframed, propped carelessly against the brick chimney, that painting was our homestead centerpiece, our newfound family grail. The first bats were out, darting black shapes in the graying sky, swooping through their accustomed hunt zone, snapping up night insects that dared to fly in that corridor along the garden. The artist was off on a twilight walk, but there in the half-light, his towel hung from the black cherry tree. The little tent was pitched again, just where it stood the night before.

Chapter 5

THE RUSTIC CABIN

Annie and I had bought the cabin when Blake was just short of his second birthday, a young couple fleeing the city with our first child. We hadn't figured on an area quite that remote, but Rita Lonborg of Pinewoods Regional High School was the only principal who'd agreed to hire us both – I would teach English, Annie Science. And if that weren't enough to sway us, Pinewoods had excellent daycare for faculty children, right there on school grounds.

We also hadn't figured on a house quite that far into the backwoods. It was remote even by Pinewoods Regional standards. But it struck us right away as very different from the rest, a cottage in a sort of magical pine kingdom, though a cottage under a spell and gone badly to seed. The land, the trees, the pond across the road, the lake back behind – it was a setting we could never have imagined. The rustic log cabin, set on the back shoulder of a gentle incline, was something out of a storybook. A gambrel roof shod with hand-split shingles draped the front of the house. It dropped steeply at first, then angled out, supported by thick log posts to form the porch roof. This gave the house a fairy tale look, but cast its lower section into a gloom of perpetual shadow, an effect much worsened by its immediate surroundings – great boulders, some lurching up from the earth and others piled to a post-glacial effect;

piles of garbage and loosely sorted scrap; and the waist-high weeds and stunted saplings that managed to grow in the gaps. Annie, though, was ever the optimist, ever the visionary. She saw a lawn and garden and flowers in their place. And, forever over-estimating my carpentry skills, she figured I'd add an open-air deck and a few second-floor windows in front to cheer the place up.

The cabin itself was solid and seamless, the work of a professional log cabin crew. But the second floor interior was so appalling it had to have been done after the fact, by a hapless owner whose funds had run dry along the way. An unfinished labyrinth of dividing walls formed four cramped bedrooms around a tiny bathroom. The ceilings were oppressively low and held a single bare bulb in each room. Every third nail was badly driven and bent over itself. And the sheetrocking was the strangest thing in the house. It was set horizontally, and only from the knees to the shoulders, with gaping voids above and below. The see-through effect into the bedrooms was comic at first, but the more we thought about it the creepier it got, in a hillbilly sort of way. Wiring ran naked beneath the sheetrock's lower edges, passing through studs set more sparsely than convention, or code, would dictate. Shingle nails pierced through the plywood roof. There was very little sunlight. It felt more like a shed than a house up there. A beaver lodge was more thoroughly constructed, and probably less depressing in its upper chambers.

But it was a place we could actually afford. The sellers were Braxton and Angela Bethune – Braxton, a small-jawed, jittery man; and Angela a bespectacled, wide-hipped woman who never said more than a word or two in all our dealings. They were selling without an agent, showing the house themselves, which made things more awkward than they might have been. Their grown son, Bobby, the holdover – his twin brother and older sister had moved out years earlier – would walk out of the room the moment we entered. Hungry-lean and wearing a dirty-blonde mullet, he'd appear in the next room too, and the next, as if waiting for us, just for the fleeting moment, only to vanish again. When I did happen to catch his eyes, they were full of resentment. They were the kind you come across every once in a while, the kind that tell you, beyond any emotion of the moment, that he's a little crazy on a full-time basis. I discussed it with Annie afterwards, and she agreed that something in certain people's eyes – a wild gleam, a manic displaced focus – could give you that impression, and that impression always seemed to pan out in the long run.

I did feel bad for him – it was probably the only house he'd ever lived in. On the other hand, he was well beyond old enough to have moved on in life. And, in the end, if Annie and I didn't buy the house, somebody else would. Mr. Bethune let on that the family needed money quickly, in consideration of some pressing obligation he pointedly would not discuss. Not that we expected him to discuss it, or to let on, as he did, that he hadn't had a single offer. The school term was nearly upon us. In our own blissful ignorance, we were happy to take the project at a hefty discount. I politely declined his offer to provide upstairs finish work for an extra consideration.

We got our loan on employment letters from Rita Lonborg. Annie's sister Clare, a couple years out of law school, helped us through the paperwork. The next thing we knew, we owned the place. We bought an old pickup, and traded in the only car I'd ever owned for salvage. Living in the city, mostly biking and walking, I'd gone weeks at a time without driving that car. But it still showed a very respectable two hundred and thirteen thousand miles when we gave it up. In twelve years of ownership, I'd never officially washed it. Wet snow pushed like a sponge would lift the city grime a couple times a winter, but the official streak became a point of pride. Pigeon droppings on the dull navy finish were marks of honor, milky symbols of the bike lover's disregard for his auto – though I was happy enough every time it started up for a weekend away. When I left the lot I was surprised to feel like I'd just put my old dog down, like the frontier boy Travis when he shot Old Yeller.

Our last night in the city, Clare arrived with a bottle of wine and insisted on christening our "new" truck – it had one hundred forty-seven thousand miles. "Look at these. They're so cute," she said, pulling three stick figure family decals from an ugly lavender gift bag. "You can customize your whole family, though for the life of me I couldn't find any mommy and daddy hockey players." The customization seemed quite limited actually, two nondescript parents and a genderless baby, three white stick people stuck in a line on the back window, a bit of suburban kitsch for the countryside.

Chapter 6

DOMINION OF THE PINES

Blake and I started the next morning with another pot-banging reveille, but the artist, once again, was not there to hear it. The yard was vacant, but we knew this time to look for his things on the porch. There along the wall was the folded tent, with the empty easel and a neat pile of items he'd left behind. Breakfast on the porch was quiet – I suppose we were keeping an unspoken vigil, a furtive watch on the road. The dew was lifting quickly, leaving waist-high shrouds of mist above the tar, on the shoulder, and in the cuts in the wood to the north and west. The cat was doing its balance beam act on the deck railing, walking one length, turning the corner, walking another, and, where the rail died at the post, spinning in place and heading back again.

Almost on cue, the artist came striding into view, through the mist, with the same easy gait, the same straw hat, collarless button-down shirt, and shapeless brown trousers. Blake and I stayed seated at our breakfasts. I wasn't going to stand, only to have him walk by me again. But this time he was the first to speak:

"The morning has brought its fruits."

And with that he pulled two cloth bundles from his rucksack. He set them on the table and unwrapped, first, what had to be three cups of wild blackberries. Second came half that many raspberries, still

33

glistening with dew. Blake, who'd always been like a little bear around fresh berries, dove right in.

"Please enjoy of these while I sketch for the afternoon painting," said the artist. With Blake's cheeks already bloated with berries, the comment was moot, but delivered proudly nonetheless. "Eat as many as you'd like."

He'd spent the previous day on the painting begun on the sudden inspiration of dawn. This day's work would be the late afternoon view he'd originally intended. While we chewed on our breakfasts, he stretched another canvas and began the sketch. It was a stunning morning, full of promise, and we all enjoyed its quiet. In time, Blake slowed his berry consumption enough to rejoin the world.

"Mister Willem, I saw some purple on the trees this morning."

Good for him, I thought. I had forgotten to look.

The artist glanced at the boy. "Very good, and yes, yes, purples, browns and grays."

The sketch was already taking shape. The perspective was very similar to yesterday's.

"Are you drawing the trees all over again?"

"Yes, Master Blake, but in different light. We'll call yesterday's *White Pines on a Summer Morning*. Today's might be *White Pines Before the Dusk*." He didn't seem particularly creative with his titles.

"What's dusk?"

"Dusk is the end of the day, the time when the sun has just disappeared behind the trees."

"Why do you call them white pines when you paint them purple?"

"That's just the name of the tree, Blake," I said.

The artist considered this for a moment. "But you make a point, Master Blake." He paused again. "Would you rather we call yesterday's *Pine Trees on a Summer Morning*?"

Blake nodded and went back to his toast and berries.

"I think that might be better," said the artist.

Blake and I kicked a ball around while the artist sketched. When he'd finished and tucked his easel out of the sun, I suggested a quick tour of the property. There were many hours before he'd paint, and he seemed content enough to accept the offer. Blake, as was his custom, would lead the way. He booted the ball back toward the house and skipped across the yard. We followed his blue and green stripes into the woods.

Traces of old footpaths had fanned across our fifteen acres when we'd bought the land. I'd tidied them up over time, cutting back the undergrowth and removing fallen branches until the walks were relatively untroubled. Blake was delighted to be leading our single file. The artist, next in line, was on constant watch, his head tilting right, left, and up, for long stretches up, clearing the occasional root and managing bends in the path without so much as a look, his farmer's hat thrown rakishly back to clear his view. I found myself looking where he looked.

One path ran parallel to the road, from the edge of the yard down to the stream. Near the corrugated metal culvert it cut sharply to the south, following the water directly away from the road. The woods were thick in that section, a clutter of hardwoods growing thin and gangly in their desperate reach for the sun, and of white pines, stunted adolescents or saplings beneath a sprinkling of towering adults. The path followed the boulder-strewn creek for half a mile, climbing gently along the bank to a twenty-foot ridge that flattened and ran for some distance. Twenty paces in, the place took on a remote and dreamy feel. It was the sudden dominion of the great pines, ruling here at the exclusion of all other vegetation. The forest floor was a tawny padding of their needles, draped several inches thick, broken only by the occasional upthrust boulder or the thick yellow-gray trunks of pine. Membership in this stand required trunks four or five feet in diameter, the lowest branches twenty feet up, the highest well out of view. The impression was that of a great, thick-posted, high-ceilinged cathedral, no hint of a sky, no sound but for the nails of unseen squirrels skittering far overhead, and the creek jabbering over rocks in its low-lying bed. Some of the pines poked from the creek banks at awkward angles but shot quickly to true vertical, standing as tall and proud as those more favorably placed.

Blake and I were still enthralled by this dominion of the pines after countless visits over the span of our few years here. The artist, seeing it for the first time, froze in his tracks. His head rotated on his shoulders as if he were some strange man-bird, his hips and feet following at odd intervals. He produced a pad and pencil from some deep pocket and began to sketch at superhuman speed, flipping pages and walking with his eyes everywhere but in front of him. Without that sixth sense he would certainly have walked off the cliff. He sketched at least a dozen different views, and finger-framed at least as many more, appearing to commit them to some sort of mental photo file. Then he fell into a different sort of reverie, pocketing the pad and simply pacing back and forth, like a big restless cat. Blake and I watched him as if he were one. Blake, for his part, waited with uncharacteristic patience through the whole process until the artist settled and returned to us. I expected the artist to spout a little praise for this wonder of the wood, but he didn't actually say a word. I remember wondering why exactly that surprised me. Blake and I took our cues and resumed the walk without speaking.

Our property lines were unmarked and more or less irrelevant, but at some point we passed into the Parenteaus' twenty acres. The forest floor grew thick with ferns, many of them full and sprawling, others still unfurling as if in perpetual springtime. As we drew near, the lake hinted at itself, sparkling between branches at certain turns, then disappearing again. As we popped at last from the trees to the water's edge, Blake and I pulled to a halt. The artist began again to pace, and to frame, and to sketch, as he'd done before, peering down the shorelines in both directions, looking directly across and then back into the woods. "Maybe we can borrow Karl's pontoon, and you can paint the views from the middle of the lake," I offered. He pulled off his hat by way of an answer, brushed a hand several times over his short crop of hair, then sat abruptly on a log and stared out at the water. The sun was just up over the trees – the glare on parts of the lake was blinding. Blake climbed crab-style on the rocks. The artist produced a pipe and a pouch, and shortly we smelled the fine incense of tobacco.

He would puff that pipe on the return walk and for much of the day, until the middle afternoon would bring the light he'd seen his first day on the deck. The Parenteau boys dropped in at lunchtime. They went right to the mantel to check out the new painting. After a couple minutes – it may have been the longest I'd ever seen them not talking – Kevin asked, "What's WG?"

"Those are his initials, dumbass," said Koby.

"But what do they stand for?" Jamie asked.

"Willem is his first name," I said. "You'll have to ask him about the G."

"He's Mister Willem," said Blake, heading outside with the rest of them. I cranked out grilled cheese sandwiches for everyone, missing what I imagined to be a pretty curious conversation as they all lounged around with the artist. By the time lunch was served, they seemed already to have accepted "Mister Willem" as one of our gang. We circled our Adirondacks, and mealtime had all the normal banter. But afterwards we were more quiet, stuffed and lethargic and baking in the sun. The ketchup crusting on Kevin's cheek drew remarkably little comment. The cat made its rounds, working its way through the group, accepting pats and head scratches from each of us in turn. Early on, Annie and I had identified it as an American Shorthair, but we'd never named it, referring to it only as "the cat." Blake later dubbed it Tiger, with respect to the handsome black stripes on its silver coat and the brilliant white on its paws, chest and chin. It was an athletic cat, lightning quick, a natural hunter just entering its physical prime. It carried itself with assurance through the people it knew, working pats and scratches, and moving finally to the stranger.

Perhaps unfamiliar with cats, the artist was not forthcoming with his affections. One hand worked his pipe, the other lay frozen on his armrest. The cat would not abide this, rubbing against the artist's leg, pacing around the chair, and then, quite suddenly, leaping into the man's lap. The artist's eyes went wide. He stiffened, lowering his eyes to watch his tormentor without risking the movement of dropping his chin. His fingers clenched the armrest while the cat began to circle.

"She likes you," said Blake. The Parenteau boys had a good laugh at that.

The cat settled in on the artist's lap, facing away from him, sphinx-like, but definitely not purring, and working its needle-like front claws, with a studied nonchalance, through the fabric of the shapeless brown trousers. Very gingerly, the artist lifted his free hand, venturing a pat.

Chapter 7

A SHINIER PURPOSE

The morning of the move we piled our stuff high and tied it down with rope. It was not a job we did particularly well. Annie and I had been hockey players, not scouts or sailors. We could tie a skate lace, and a pretty solid square knot, but the more intricate stuff – the bowline, the tautline hitch, the clove hitch – knots I imagined might actually keep our things on the truck, were beyond us. We did what we could, and on a sweltering weekday afternoon in August, we puttered out to the country, fifteen miles below the speed limit. Up hills we were even slower. "The Beverly Hillbillies in reverse," Annie said. She hummed the theme song every time some traffic-crazed driver busted around us. The ropes stretched and sagged. The furniture lurched and leaned. But miraculously, nothing fell out. Annie was still humming when we pulled into the driveway some two hours later.

Cleaning up the lot seemed strangely critical to morale. Before we'd even finished unpacking we spent the better part of two days loading the truck and hauling out to the town landfill – to the degree you can take on that kind of project with a toddler in tow. As we added our unsightly scrap metal to the larger communal pile, I took a solemn moment to commemorate my faithful car, declaring it now bound, like this scrap, for some shinier purpose. Annie laughed, and this was always reward enough for me. But as the week went on, she picked up on the phrase, adopting it as a kind of tag-line for our move. Holding up a piece of junk from the yard, she'd say, "Think we can find a shinier purpose for this?" Or, "Jason, if you're looking for a shinier purpose, can you hand me that box?" She had a gift that way, an innovative approach to language, coining new phrases or making up words when conventional vocabulary fell short. On the landfill road, as we passed a house almost fully obstructed by earthmoving equipment – a backhoe, a bulldozer, a truck and a trailer all parked out front – she said, "We should try that guy and see if he'll deboulder the yard for us."

When we'd finished clearing the lot I took the sledgehammer to the labyrinth upstairs. "Jason has a bad case of demolition fever," I heard her tell Clare on the phone. And she was right – that sort of work was right down my alley. I bashed out the hillbilly sheetrock, and every section of low-slung ceiling and the dividing walls that held them, leaving only the bathroom chamber and the gaping stairwell to break the expanse of pine floorboards. She'd been hanging the pots and pans off the kitchen beam, but she came up to take a picture just then. Shafts of light from the six-over-six windows at the end of the house sliced through the demolition dust. I stood with a sepia effect in the margins of that light, holding the sledgehammer in my sweat and filth like John Henry, the steel-driving man. That photo still hangs on the wall, and I consider it from time to time, trying to recall what things were like then, what I was like then.

We were both exhausted, but we decided on a late afternoon swim in the lake, and then a campfire to close out the day. I dug a firepit in front of the house. It was a makeshift affair at first, a shallow hole, four feet in diameter, carved with a garden spade. But Annie joined in, her hair still wet from the lake, gathering some stones and fashioning them into a handsome little ring around the border. I hauled in some log sections good for sitting and set them just outside the perimeter. And just like that we had a real firepit. We spent the evening under the stars, around our own private campfire in our own private wilderness, flame leaping from the nail-laden studs. Blake snoozed in the carseat we'd set in the grass, his little face aglow at his mother's knee.

The next morning we loaded up any demo materials unfit for burning and hauled them to the landfill. Annie still had debouldering on her mind, and, at last, on the way back from our final trip, we stopped at the earthmoving house. Behind all the equipment and hidden from the road, a litter of kittens played around a tiny apple tree. One of them had worked itself onto a low branch. Blake lay in the grass as close to them as he dared. A tall, stooped, middle-aged man with a prominent nose came to the door. He identified himself as Charlie Beanland, and, yes, he would entertain prospects for work. He also offered us a kitten, and I think he was surprised when Annie accepted on the spot. Blake chose the one up the tree. Annie made it comfortable in the truck, and Charlie followed us home to take a look at the project. Blake splayed on the wood floor to watch the kitten lap its milk while Charlie and I made our deal. We sealed it with a handshake.

At 7:00 the next morning we heard him clanking the heavy chains on the trailer. Before I'd even pulled on my jeans, he'd fired up the backhoe. Like Mike in what would become one of Blake's favorite books – *Mike Mulligan and His Steamshovel* – he was something to watch, a man in perfect tandem with his machine. A one-man band in overalls, he worked both arms and both legs with a tangle of levers and pedals, his cabin swirling and his bucket in perpetual motion, a tireless beast digging and lifting, poking and probing, combing and cajoling. He dug out every boulder but one. That he abandoned, with profuse apologies, after half an hour of exertion. He and Annie reckoned it extended a good way to the earth's core. Under Annie's direction, he set the rest of the boulders, some of them nearly waist-high, in a neat row at the edge of the forest. She signalled him in theatrically, like a flight deck marshall waving light wands. He seemed to get a kick out of that, and he cooperated good-naturedly, placing each boulder as carefully as he could. She wirebrushed them until they shone almost white in the sun.

The next day he cranked up the bulldozer and started to mold and grade the earth. The outline of a yard began to take form, playing-field flat but for a nearly imperceptible drainage grade. I hadn't known it, but it occurred to me then that this was what I'd always wanted – not a fancy car, or a swimming pool, or a 10,000-foot house, but a yard big enough to catch a frisbee on the full gallop. "I can already see the frisbees flying," Annie said. Mindreading was one of her most distinctive traits. Charlie was done in two days, just as he'd said. The lawn was going to be perfect. I wrote him a check, and Annie sent him home with a roasted chicken. The new school year began the next day.

Chapter 8

PINE TREES BEFORE THE DUSK

We awoke to a few gifts the next morning. The cat had left a chipmunk on the doormat, the kind of offering it made at intervals in lieu of rent. And the artist had collected three different bird nests on his early walk. He displayed them on the arms of three chairs he'd set in a row. The cat would often behead its prey, and I would hide those offerings from Blake. But this chipmunk was intact, with no visible injuries, peaceful in death. The three of us admired its brilliant white underbelly and the smart striping down its back as I explained the cat's intent to contribute to the household.

"You mean she wants us to eat it?"

"Yes, but we don't eat chipmunks like she does. So we put it back in the woods when she's not looking, and she thinks we ate it. That way we don't hurt her feelings."

The artist gave me a look of indignation, as if I were stuffing the boy with nonsense. He muttered quietly in a language he knew I couldn't understand. This struck me as funny, and I broke into laughter, which seemed to outrage him all the more. Maintaining his dignity and reserve, he turned the conversation to the nests. They were all "cup nests" as he described them. Each was beautifully formed of grassy materials, but they varied in overall size and depth and in the

43

types of grass and weaving, and in the prevalence and types of bonding materials. Blake held the first nest with great reverence, cupping his hands in front of him as if he were taking communion. The artist pulled that nest and replaced it with another, explaining that birds often used saliva to bond their nests, and sometimes, he claimed, even spider silk. "Spider subcontractors," I quipped. Neither Blake nor the artist even pretended to smile.

Besides the nests, he had gathered more berries, and was happy to accept "a modicum" of cornbread and honey in return. He ventured a comment on Blake's appetite for berries, calling him "the little cub." We sat three in a row, facing out to the trees and, beyond them, to the pond. As the meal wound down the artist began to stare out with a different kind of hunger. He'd been able to relax a bit between the paintings, but with a work in progress – he'd gotten in maybe five hours late the day before – any daylight hour spent idly seemed to grate at him. This was especially the case, I imagined, when we were staring at his subject vista over our breakfasts. I stood to clear the plates. He accepted his cue to set up the easel and the canvas he'd begun to paint the day before. Blake and I seized the opportunity for subtle peeks.

The trees of his afternoon light had already come into their colors. They were the same trees, viewed from the same vantage point, but they were only distant relations of the morning versions, more shimmery, as if seen through a haze of summer heat that left one faint and dreamy. They showed no trace of purple, swimming instead in yellows and grays. I would have sat there for the rest of the day to watch him finish that painting, and I imagine Blake would have too but for the series of scowls and grunts from the artist. It was clear by now he was not fond of an audience.

Blake and I packed lunches and dressed for a day on the lake. As we headed out, toting our paddles and poles, I told the artist he had a sandwich waiting for him in the fridge. For a man of few words, he was effusive in his thanks. He ended with "You are very kind," and another of his little bows. You had to respect his sincerity. This kind of simple gesture – an offered sandwich, a house left open, quiet time to work – seemed to go far with him.

Blake and I retraced the property tour we'd taken with the artist the day before. It was the long way to the lake, but the dominion of the pines had that kind of pull. Blake led us through as he always did, but I noticed a slight change in the way he looked at the trees that morning, a slight increase in his focus. We stored the canoe at lakeside, upside down and partially concealed in the undergrowth. I flipped it, pulled it into the water and held it steady as Blake, in his lifejacket and little red water shoes, worked his way to the front, stepping gingerly over the thwarts. When he was set I shoved us off. Lake minnows scattered from the boat. Blake had to kneel way up in the prow to reach his extra-short paddle into the water. His skinny arms went hard to work. Forty meters out he had me stop paddling for a bit, to see if he could propel the boat by himself. It seemed that he really could keep us moving, and I threw a string of compliments in with the occasional silent paddle stroke. But he soon tired or lost interest, and halfway to the island we drifted to a standstill. It was rote behavior, when sitting motionless in a canoe, to throw out our fishing lines. So we did that too, though it was the wrong time of day. We may have had a nibble, but didn't catch a thing. We weren't much disappointed.

We knew the little island very well, with its three oversized pines and surrounding scrub. Overheated from our exposure in the canoe, we leapt right off the jumping rock with no fear of the cold. Blake dog-paddled from rock to rock, his life jacket riding up under his chin. A big flat rock shelf on the island's southern edge made for a perfect sunning surface and, later, when we were dry and warm, a perfect spot for a picnic. Stranded little batches of lake water filled depressions in the stone and went hot in the sun. We watched a loon dive and dip while we ate, and just after lunch a great grey heron passed overhead. I noticed the moon was up.

Six or seven turtles sunned on a log. Blake tossed a stone near them, and they all slipped into the water. We waited to see if they'd climb back on, and when we lost interest I started skipping stones while Blake counted the hops. We swam again and sunned again, and when Blake's jacket was dry I buckled it on him and shoved us off for home. "The turtles are back," he said. They were just as before, half a dozen all in a row.

It was mid-afternoon when we got back to the cabin. The artist manned his post on the deck. He was intent, bent to his work, the watchmaker, the surgeon, the royal goldsmith setting the queen's gemstones. The nod he gave us was less a greeting than a flag of panic, so intense was his fear of an interruption at that moment. I reined in my nosiness, and Blake was so overdue for his nap that his nosiness was already on hold. I put a wet cloth to his face and neck, gave him a drink, and fed him some grapes. We lay on the daybed, closing our eyes to the subtle sounds of the artist at work. I could tell when his brush was near the bottom of the canvas – the awkward bending would make his breathing short and labored. He must have straightened up just then, as his breathing smoothed out, and his brush, barely audible on the canvas, resumed its more contented pace. He sighed now at intervals, the coo of the mourning dove. Blake was fast asleep.

I awoke some time later to the rumble of thunder. I don't know how long we'd slept, but the skies over the pond were dark and heavy, and moving fast. I lifted Blake from the daybed, his head rotating instinctively to a comfortable spot on my shoulder, his body heated with sleep. The artist scurried over to hold the door for us, then scampered back to rescue his work from the wind. The first droplets were already spotting the deck. Just as I'd transferred Blake to his bed, a crack of thunder ushered in the storm. It was the kind of thunder that usually sent him scampering around the house, howling in a manic blend of glee and terror, the kind of thunder no one could possibly sleep through, except Blake after a day on the lake. As the rain pelted down I went outside to check on the artist. He'd pulled his easel under the porch roof and secured the canvas, draped and tied in cloth, against the house. I pulled up an Adirondack for each of us.

"I'm sorry we can't give you a little better weather today."

He didn't answer for what seemed like the longest time, but I'd learned to expect a wait. "I enjoy a storm," he said at last. And then, after another pause, "You are very kind for me to camp here. The light and trees are very good for painting."

"Not today," I said. The sky was almost black. "But it's been fun watching you work. Although we try not to really watch. I imagine it's a bit intrusive. Your work is superb."

He sat silently again. This time, I thought the conversation was actually over. "You are kind to say so," he said. "I enjoy painting in this knee of the woods."

"You mean this neck of the woods."

"Why neck?"

"That's just the expression. Why knee?"

"I thought it to mean a bend in the land. It would appear like a knee on the map."

"Probably makes more sense than neck," I said. He was silent then, and I was happy to let it rest. It was the snappiest conversation we'd had to date.

"I mean for you to keep the painting," he said suddenly.

I was shocked. "You mean the one on the mantel? *White Pines on a Summer Morning?*"

"No, Master Blake was correct. It is *Pine Trees on a Summer Morning.*"

"Ah, yes," I smiled. "Well, it's very nice of you. It's a beautiful work, fantastic really, and it's perfect on our mantel. But I can't keep it. You need to sell it. Don't you sell your paintings?"

He seemed disappointed, perhaps even offended.

"For god's sake Willem, it should be in a museum somewhere. If I had the money I'd definitely buy it." I had a sudden sinking feeling and began a quick internal inventory. How much would a painting like that be worth, and how could we afford it? "I just mean, well, you need the money don't you? You paint for a living, no?" Here I weathered a long pause.

"I live to paint. Little is sold, and little matter of it. I have no place to hold my work."

"I can hold paintings for you here if you want. You can sell them whenever you're ready."

"I mean for you to keep the painting." He was deadly serious.

"OK, Willem. OK. We'll keep it. Right where it is, on the mantel." He seemed to breathe a little easier. "And thank you," I added. "It's fantastic." And I meant it. He seemed relieved, and, selfishly, I was thrilled to have the painting. Beside our land, it was by far the nicest thing Blake and I had ever owned. At the same time, I was horrified for the artist, wandering around, living in a tent, giving away ridiculously good work, work too good to let go at almost any price. I knew I shouldn't press the point, but I couldn't help myself.

"Don't you need the money?"

This time he didn't answer at all, and it didn't really surprise me. Maybe he was self-sufficient, even wealthy, off now on some lark. Maybe he was as he appeared, dirt poor, living day to day. All I knew is that he wouldn't say.

We sat for some time then, watching the rain spatter on the road, the sky flashing bright and then dark again as we waited for what had become more distant rumbles. The artist murmured quietly after every flash of lightning. It was a language I didn't understand, but after a while I realized that he was counting to the thunder, as a child might, gauging the distance of the storm. By this time water was running in ruts down the driveway. I was surprised to see him suddenly so relaxed, enjoying the view. We pulled our chairs to the edge of the porch roof to see as much of the sky as we could without getting soaked. The show was spectacular but short-lived as the storm raced off to the west. It cleared out so quickly I had the same feeling, like watching some old film clip running at triple speed, as when I'd first seen him sketching. The sun popped out like someone had flipped the master switch. The asphalt road, baked earlier by hours of summer heat, steamed off the rainfall. By the time Blake awoke from his nap there was almost no sign of it. The clouds were suddenly sparse, white again, and fluffy. The artist stood back to his work.

Blake, when he'd cleared the cobwebs, was anxious to make up for the time lost napping. He heard the familiar sound of bouncing basketballs at the end of the driveway, and we headed up to join the Parenteaus' shootaround. He was too little to shoot but happily retrieved any loose ball, bouncing it with two hands, sometimes into a puddle, before passing it off to one of the Parenteau boys. Jamie was always mindful to include Blake. He'd act the part of the beleaguered defender when Blake had the ball, leaving both of them giggling as I patrolled behind, trying to keep the other boys' rebounds from landing on their heads.

The artist worked until nearly dark. I was ready for him this time when he came to the screen, but he surprised me by looking for the cat and handing me the canvas through the doorway, indicating how to grasp it so my fingers wouldn't smudge the paint. I set the painting next to the first one on the mantel, then made some adjustments, trying to get the spacing between them just right. The artist went back for the easel, which he laid against the house.

This was our first authorized look. We'd given the artist more space this time, and he'd been an aggressive defender when we'd been on his perimeter, draping the canvas under cloth when he wasn't standing in front of it. But with the painting now completed he was more than happy for us to see it. The brighter the light – and this painting was set in a midsummer's afternoon – the ghostlier were his pines, night creatures caught creeping by day. The trunks were vertically-laid mosaics, draped in knobby yellow shrouds – full of faint, half-submerged faces with gaping mouths and startled eyes – and sprouting ill-formed limbs just before rising off the canvas. They seemed to flee before a sky that brought not just the threat of weather, but of a general malevolence, a certain cruel mastery. A boulder in the foreground gave the effect of its true gray, but as if seen through a magical prism and broken into all its tiny components, spots from half a dozen colors gathered like a funeral bouquet. And the road just behind was not the crumbled, shoddy asphalt I saw by day, but a byway to any number of possible outcomes, a shimmering and loose-shaped stream to anywhere.

Pine Trees on a Summer Morning. Pine Trees Before the Dusk. I was beginning to like the look of that room.

Chapter 9

THE HOMESTEADERS

On a glorious sunny Saturday, the first of our new school year, Annie and I spread the seeds of our dream lawn. We raked out the tracks of Charlie's bulldozer, then doubled back and fine-raked the whole clearing. By mid-afternoon there wasn't a pebble larger than a kernel of corn in a field of soil so rich and smooth and fluffy we hated even to walk on it. Wherever we went we dragged the rakes behind us, scratching out our tracks the instant they'd been formed. Late in the afternoon, we seeded with an old-school hand-spreader, taking turns walking barefoot down invisible rows, turning the crank that twirled the seed in tan vortexes to the earth. "Just like churning butter," Annie said, though we both knew she'd never done any such thing. We hand-watered at twilight, one of us maneuvering the body of the hose, the other directing a fine and uniform mist, just enough to darken the soil to a coffee brown without puddling. We watered like that every day thereafter, before school and again at the end of the day, watching the dirt like starving homesteaders for the first shoots of green. In a couple of weeks we had a fine fuzzy overlay. In just over a month we had something of a lawn, a small patch in front of the house and the great expanse to the side, running back toward the stream.

I bought a push mower at Jerry's Country Equipment and cranked it up for its first run. Halfway in, Charlie happened to drive by, honked over the roar of the mower, and waved. Just like that, life had become "the never-ending long weekend," as we called it. Was this a conceivable reality, waking into such an existence, seven days a week? We'd stroll onto the porch with coffee in our hands and the first sun in the trees, and Annie would say, "How's this for a shinier purpose?" We'd loved the city, but at some point every day you couldn't help but flee from it, from the traffic and noise, the ugly streets and bad air. We'd stagger into the four-wall enclave of our apartment, dead-bolt the door, drop onto the couch, and sigh in relief. Now we lived in our own private reserve, a period piece cabin with log walls, and floors and ceilings of pine, everything scented of the forest. The windows were brilliant works of ever-changing art, framed views out into the fantastic light and color of the coming autumn foliage.

As delightful as cabin life could be, every minute spent indoors was carefully scrutinized, harshly assessed by the committee of one. We'd be sitting happily at the table and Annie would suddenly say, "What possible reason do we have to be inside right now?" Out we'd go, throwing sweaters over our heads, and funny hats and fuzzy body suits on Blake, for meals or snacks or backgammon on the porch. The sun poured around us, leaving the world translucent and aglow in its seasonal citrus – the bright green of the brand new lawn, the yellow, orange and red of the leaves. We read books aloud, nestled on the daybed, children's books to Blake and our own favorites to each other.

Nightfall was a show all its own, often viewed from the edges of our private firepit, with a starscape so ridiculous we could only laugh. For a reasonably educated person I found I knew almost nothing about what went on overhead. The Big Dipper and Orion's Belt were about the only constellations I could find and name, though in all that glitter I figured they were all up there somewhere. A lifetime in the city had also retarded my understanding of the moon and its movements. After a withering cross-examination Annie determined that I was "oblivious, completely oblivious" to the fact that its rising time changed by half an hour every night in our part of the world, and that sometimes, therefore, it even rose in the morning. I'd seen it up in the day, of course, but to her great amazement, I'd never quite grasped the concept. She introduced the cycles of the moon, immediately, into her Pinewoods Regional earth science curriculum.

We explored the forest like city kids on the march with Lewis and Clark. We collected leaves and pressed them into a book: a catalogue of hardwoods, whole ranges of oak and maple and beech; a dozen or more conifers, led by the majestic white pine; and the paper-barked, fairy-white birch, which seemed an order all to itself. Annie introduced this exercise into her curriculum as well, a fall project requiring her students to collect and identify two dozen local leaves. She reported their moaning pathetically at the prospect, but they didn't seem all that unhappy when we'd actually come across them in the woods. We'd be hiking up the old logging road, Blake stuffed into his padded pack, feet hanging out at my sides, and they'd all smile and fuss over him. Dozens of trails branched off that long-abandoned double-rut path, some dying abruptly in the brush, others running on for miles. Over those first months we marked a host of trailheads and nicknamed the best of them — Blackberry Bend, Uproot, Birch Grove, Tightrope. We bought topography maps one after another at Jerry's Country Equipment, tacking them together on the kitchen wall, expanding sector by sector.

We'd trade off late afternoons, each of us freed on alternate days for as long a ride as we could handle. One day, I'd top off her tires and send her off, watching her zip down our road, clearing the culvert, leaning into the beaver pond bend, straightening, shrinking, and gone. The next day's ride was mine. I'd clip in where the gravel drive met the paved road – a couple quick pedals on the slight initial downhill and

I was launched into the country. This was what cycling was all about, not some half-speed city trail dodging around baby strollers and dogs on leashes, but full-out thigh-busting runs through miles of wilderness paradise. Our route was generally to the north, over two covered bridges, past the state line and up toward the mountains, as far as we thought we could go and make it back without wilting. At the end of the rides my quads would be so distended I could hardly walk. I'd step off my bike and stagger around like a drunk until my legs reached equilibrium. Annie, with Blake at her shoulder, always seemed to be there, just at those moments, to share the laugh.

The first hints of northern chill forced our attentions to an issue we'd been steadfastly ignoring: the cabin had no heat beyond the woodstove. The good news was there was no end of fallen timber to section and haul. I went back to Jerry's Country Equipment and bought my first chainsaw. We joked about this, my rite of manly passage. But if we were going to occupy the second floor, we had to insulate the ceiling – the Bethunes had survived largely on space heaters up there. So we moved the crib downstairs, and we worked together, a few hours a night, as quietly as we could. We built scaffolds of sawhorses and planks. We rolled the insulation into the gaps between the joists, stapled the securing strips, and covered it all with sections of thin plywood. By the first snow, the woodstove could keep the whole house warm. We were real northern country folk, settled in for the cold.

Chapter 10

GARDEN AT NOON WITH FIGURE

Early the next morning the artist was asking about the trails further up the old logging road. After the normal pause for his shoe removal, I took him inside so he could study the topography maps. There were twelve of them in all, pieced together, but not in a neat four-by-three grid. The arrangement was irregular, like an unfinished puzzle, chasing the most hikable topography, the thousands of forested acres that jogged to the north and west, high up our kitchen wall. Annie's markings were all over those maps, a hand-sketched cabin the size of a Monopoly house and colored highlighters marking the paths we'd hiked, each named on a separate key with corresponding colors. I described a few of the trails and the stones we'd set to mark them.

Pointing with one finger, the artist quickly worked out where he'd been on his walks. He pulled the pad and pencil from his pocket – he was apparently never without them – and sketched a copy for himself. Emboldened within the walls of my own house, I looked brazenly over his shoulder while he drew. He didn't seem to mind, just as he hadn't when he'd sketched on the napkin. His resentment that way seemed limited to works on canvas. What I saw taking shape this time was a quick reduction of the whole trail network, impeccably calibrated and far more pleasing than the standardized presentation of the U.S.

Geographical Survey. He flipped the page way before I was done admiring it, and started in on a more detailed cutout, a section of critical forkways drawn in a much larger scale and just as skillfully rendered. Both sketches were perfectly positioned and perfectly proportioned, filling their respective pages without threatening to overrun at any edge. When he closed the pad I had half a mind to grab it, just like I'd grabbed the napkin, but, perhaps wiser for the incident, he tucked it away.

"I used to keep a book just like that," I said in penance for my larcenous thoughts. I pulled mine out of a kitchen drawer, showed it quickly, and shoved it back in. The two books were even more similar than I'd imagined, both just small enough to fit in a large pocket, both with orange-brown covers. "But I don't really draw."

"What do you keep there?"

Blake called from the bathroom. I hesitated for a moment. The artist stood staring. I nodded an apology and headed out of the kitchen, muttering my answer on the move. "Plate numbers," I said. I wasn't sure if he'd heard.

When Blake and I came back out the artist was off into the woods. As a prodigious walker bent on covering new ground, I figured he'd be gone a good while. I didn't notice when he returned, probably because I was hunched over a hoe in Annie's garden. This was my second summer tending it for her. Gardening wasn't really my thing, but I figured the least I could do was keep it going that first summer. A bunch of dead plantings would have been pretty depressing. It was easy enough to keep it watered and weeded, and that was about all the energy I could muster. Fortunately, that was all that was required. The black cherry threw some afternoon shade, but overall the exposure was just about perfect. The soil was rich. Things grew. Blake seemed to like the process of planting and watering and watching things grow. And both of us liked what came later even more – picking vegetables or digging them right out of the soil to eat that same night. Blake and I never discussed it, but there was something of Annie in all of it, a kind of an ongoing gift in the form of carrots and potatoes in a bowl. The pumpkin patch was fantastic, vines shooting everywhere like some mutant man-eating strain, with big green gourds sitting idly in their beds, weeks on end, then turning picture book orange at the change of the season on the ends of their withered vines. The next spring I pitchforked in a few barrow-loads of compost and planted the garden all over again – all the same crops in just the same places.

I straightened up to settle my back, and there was the artist at the far edge of the yard, fully in shade and partially obstructed by his easel. I hollered over a greeting and he grunted back an undetermined monosyllable, though he stared at me steadily, as if he were somehow interested in my work. I bent back to the hoeing, down one row and up another, obliterating weeds and turning the soil. The cat took a mouse from the far edge of the garden. She pranced around to the front of the house, the head hanging to one side, the tail to the other. Blake had missed the catch, running back and forth across the yard, peeking naughtily at the artist's work. I unwound the hose and had him spray a fine mist of water from the edge of the deck until the garden soil had gone dark and the plants all shone and dripped.

I went in to get us drinks and stopped on the porch, where the cat was devouring her catch. It was the first time I'd really witnessed that very definitive end, the skull cracking like a walnut way back in the molars, the tail going down last, vanishing like a string of spaghetti. Blake drank his water and delivered a glass to the artist. The field needed a mow, but I was careful about jumping into too many chores during Blake's waking hours. I didn't worry so much about the only child's distress at solitude, but rather his seeming ease with it. Maybe he was getting too good at it out here, in spite of the Parenteau boys – after all, they had school nine months of the year. But he seemed particularly happy to occupy himself in the yard today. The artist at his easel on the forest edge was something new and different, for one thing. And I heard the boys in the distance – it was just a matter of time before they would wander over. So I lugged the mower out through the bulkhead and cranked it into action.

Blake skipped back and forth between more peeks at the easel and comical marches behind me while I mowed. I worried that the artist might be irritated by the combination of the mischief and the blare of the mower. But he too seemed perfectly content, working there beneath his straw hat. It was the first time I'd seen him puffing his pipe at the easel. His curtain of shade was shrinking by the minute as the sun charged over the treeline. I worked from the garden out, toward his station at the forest edge, looking back periodically to admire the manicured grass stripes in my wake. It was a big lawn for a push mower. I moved as fast as it could handle, and after twenty minutes I was in full lather. Every five or six strips I'd remove the catch, walk it double-time into the woods, dump the clippings into the compost pile and trot back. Across the drive, Karl was onto some project, hauling materials in a cart behind his tractor. The neighborhood was fairly abuzz. After a time the Parenteau boys did stroll in, Kevin's voice piercing even through the roar of the mower. I figured this might put the artist over the edge. But he seemed unfazed, from what little I could see of him poking around the easel, under his straw hat, spewing clouds of pipe smoke.

The boys fiddled around for a while, and then Jamie went inside for the frisbee. They'd gotten pretty good at catching and throwing but weren't much for doing it by themselves. They preferred me launching it out to the edge of their range so they could catch it on the full sprint. Blake liked to run after it, and sometimes I'd see him just staring at the disc in flight against the backdrop of trees. I realized they were buying time until I'd finished the mowing, so I shut it down with a few strips to go, leaving the artist on an island of long-growth. I had an idea I'd try to move the boys across the driveway into the Parenteaus' field, to leave him at peace. But our field was better for frisbee. The apple trees at the edges of their place were problematic. And on this day anyway, our grass had a feel and a scent that was hard to abandon. It was perfect underfoot. The boys had already pulled off their shoes and socks, so we settled in to play.

The artist, far from seeming irritated, stood mesmerized at the frisbee's flight, as if it were a hawk at a thousand feet, or an albatross a thousand miles to sea. As I flung a few for the boys, I noticed that he'd stepped away from the easel and was lingering at the edge of the striping. He too was suddenly barefoot. I threw him a soft one. Surprised as he seemed to see it coming his way, he caught it clean. He refused to try to throw it back, but quickstepped across the lawn and delivered it back to me directly. I showed him the grip and motioned to him to try a throw, but he would have none of it, catching but never throwing as I worked him into the rotation. The boys were getting a kick out of him. I started to stretch him out, putting the frisbee further and further out of his reach. He took a couple steps, and then broke into a run, his bare white feet shocking in contrast to his brown trousers. Soon he was making regular sprints across the lawn, losing his hat time and again and returning for it after every catch. At last he let it lie. It seemed nearly to levitate, so thick was the freshly-mowed grass beneath it.

"Nice catch, Willem," one of us would say, and the artist would run to the nearest player and hand him the frisbee. He was a natural retriever, with decent footspeed, dogged concentration, and a pretty good set of hands. His sixth sense for avoiding unseen objects served him well here. On one throw he dodged both his hat and his easel, his eyes never leaving the floating violet orb.

After an hour, the boys retired to the deck for lemonade, and the artist returned to his easel. He rekindled his pipe, mopped his brow, and set back to work, still barefoot in the sun. I had Blake deliver him a glass, and from the deck I saw him take it, bow to the boy and then to me, and gulp it down. Half a dozen robins now patrolled the lawn, attracted as always to a fresh cut.

The boys played on and around the deck for most of the rest of the afternoon. The dynamic between them was good – the Parenteau boys would fight like dogs as a threesome, but Blake seemed to have a calming effect on them. They were growing up fast, and having a four-year-old in the mix seemed like a license to be dopey and childish again. Blake had big cardboard blocks they liked to drag up from the basement, and in combination with chairs and cushions and whatever else they could muster, they had the makings of two forts. They would fire balled socks at each other inexhaustibly – socks gladly supplied by me in exchange for an hour of engagement – howling like monkeys and going red in the face. The artist labored all through the battle, and through the down time after. Late in the day, he brought the painting onto the deck. He gripped it so the back of the canvas faced us where we sat.

"Are you done already?" I asked. With the late start and the frisbee break this would be quick work indeed. We all sat silently, waiting for his answer. Not without some hint of drama, he flipped the canvas. "Garden at Noon," he said. And, in a strange aside, "with Figure."

It was the height of a midsummer's day in every dab of paint. The lawn alone swore to just that moment, thousands of tiny vertical strokes tamed and herded into manicured stripes, alternating in prevailing waves of noonish yellows and mid-day greens. And the house was as clearly spoken as a watch pointing twelve, its logs textured like animal furs, its hand-split shingles crude and uneven, almost medieval – neither turned up in the colors I'd have assigned them. They came in the palette of unrivaled sun, a sun not shown but for the coating and coloring of everything beneath. Such noons were perfectly familiar – I'd seen thousands before but had never quite grasped them, not like this. The garden burst in an orderly riot before the cabin, mottled lots of purples and browns and greens, all in praise of that same noon star. And there in that garden, lurching in the furrows, was something that could only be me, a round, hunched, toiling creature, faceless in the soil. This then was the Figure, relatively small on the canvas, but large enough, certainly, to warrant some hint of detail. Even the slightest gesture that way would have done. But instead my face was a brown blur, an insignificant and inhuman smudge, a blob with a nose. The boys were rolling with laughter.

"What the hell, Willem?" I said with mock indignation. "I take you in, feed you, throw you the frisbee, encourage your work, and this is my reward? The Figure! Where's my face? Why so fat? And what's with the giant shoes?"

The artist was flushed and somewhat flustered. "I meant no offense, Mister Jason," he said with a bow. And then he couldn't help but crack a smile.

Chapter 11

BLACK ICE

Annie and I didn't know it at the time, but our first winter in Pinewoods was a one-in-a-dozen weather event. It was pond hockey paradise, perfect and protracted. The cold came early, dry and steady. A week into December we were taking our first tentative steps on the shallow beaver pond, and by the time school broke for the holidays the whole lake was polished into black marble. The snow fell lightly when it fell at all – the wind swept it into wispy sidewinders that writhed across the ice and flew off at the shore, smoke rings hurrying into the woods.

We'd both spent countless hours in rinks – city rinks, suburban rinks, high school rinks, college rinks. We'd both ridden the buses, dressed in the dank, moldy locker-rooms, sucked a lifetime of Zamboni fumes, skated in pens of half-walls that glowed a sickly pale in the artificial light. Black ice was an entirely different experience. We'd walk up the tree-lined drive with skates and sticks slung over our shoulders, breathing steam and hearing only the crunch of the gravel under our boots. When we turned onto the woodpath we always seemed to pick up our pace – the grade was slightly downhill, and the ice had a pull on us as sure as the moon's on the tide. At the lake's edge we'd run and slide a time or two, and then set a milk crate for lacing. Annie would sit first, pulling off her mittens and racing to get her skates tied before her fingers numbed up. When I took her place on the crate, she'd flit around the cove, putting on a special little ice show. She'd mimic a figure skater doing compulsory eights, her hands balletically outstretched, her back arched, her head thrown back. She'd hold this regal arabesque for a full five-count, then skip into a little axel jump, landing on the same leg and gliding backwards, her backside tilted out just so. Then she'd grab her stick and head off, striding like a real hockey player, shrinking quickly into the distance. Only then would I begin to lace.

When I could see her looking back from a quarter mile or more, I'd fire off a low slapshot and count slowly, deliberately, to ten or twelve or fourteen, waiting for the echoed clack of it onto her stick. There was something perfect about that puck as it shot across the frictionless surface, unwavering, defying time and distance. The ice was so hard our blades would barely crease it. The silence, when we remembered to listen, was the dream of an imagined afterlife, no sound but the scratching of our blades as we skated in tandem, and the soft clacking of the puck as we passed it stick to stick. The lake offered the big sky we didn't often see in those woods, draped now in low winter light, and set all around on the distant ring of naked hardwoods.

The Parenteau boys began to follow us onto the ice, shuffling on their boots and kicking at the puck. They were suitably impressed with us – hockey was something we had both played a lot – but it was Annie who really had their attention. They were shocked to see a woman skate like that, carving on all four edges with grace and power and speed. I had a lot of old sticks in the basement and cut one down for each of them, measuring floor to nose. They played enthusiastic boot hockey for those few days until Christmas, when skates appeared under the Parenteau tree. Those skates were the product of a joint initiative between Karl and me. Karl took a yuletime leave from his chores and was perched at lakeside when the boys strapped them on that afternoon for the first time. They spent the balance of Christmas Day wobbling on their new blades, dragging their ankles and leaning on their sticks like human tripods. Kevin would head off full bore and whirl and twirl in the most entertaining fashion, his stick flying as he pitched spectacularly to the ice in his thick winter padding. Koby's own spasticity in no way hindered the stream of insults he would level at his brothers – he would often crash to the ice mid-sentence, to the general hilarity. But they stuck with it, and they started to skate, as even the most callow beginners tend to do when they're racing for pucks. Suddenly we had a pack of players.

Unless she was working a police dispatch shift, as she did a few times a week, Betty was nice enough to watch Blake while we skated. She often walked him down to the lake edge in his boots and his puffy snowsuit. When we picked him up afterwards we'd generally stay for hot chocolate. Betty loved to chat, and had access to more local news than we could imagine. By the time we shuffled up the driveway for home, sticks on our outside shoulders, Blake between us, each of his mittened hands in one of ours, the light would be fading, and we'd be dizzy with more scoop on our little community than we'd ever quite wanted. Carly Lonborg, daughter of our school principal and employer, had just finalized her third divorce, each messier than the last. The Claytons, distant neighbors around the lake, had just given birth to Down syndrome twins. And early in the year Bobby Bethune had been arrested on a break and entry, partying with some friends in a house the owners had left for the weekend. He'd busted the place up and burnt a lot of the furniture. Worse, he'd sliced up some poor kid's hamster and left it in sections on a Santa Claus serving plate. Substantial restitution had been required. This was all a little creepy, but it explained a few things for us, in particular what had prompted the Bethunes to sell us their place. We were gratified that Betty seemed more pleased with her new neighbors.

The real snows came midway through January, quiet as a thief, fluffy and deep. The great white pines held up better than we'd expected, the powder seeming to drop from their windswept limbs more easily than it did from the firs, or the spruce. Those bent, and often disappeared completely, under bundles of white that left only the suggestion of trees. You'd think being more or less snowed in for a couple months would have been a great time to settle in and knock off the indoor projects. But I didn't produce much finish work that first winter. The wood fire had a deadly charm those nights. It was nearly impossible to pull myself away from it, watching the flame through the stove glass, nestled with Annie on the couch while Blake snoozed under his quilt in the corner. It just wasn't clear on those wintry evenings that labor offered a truly shinier purpose. And the fact is, I'm a plodding carpenter. "Deliberate" was the more charitable word Annie used. With what little energy I could muster after school and on weekends, I just managed to rail in the steps, run the rough electric, and frame the two bedrooms.

The sheetrock stock was bought and paid for, stacked on the floor upstairs. We couldn't go anywhere up there without stepping around it. But it was a project I just couldn't seem to start. I'd never liked sheetrock work in the first place, and this job had one particular complication. The cabin was essentially a log box, and where the interior partition walls met the logs at right angles, I had to scribe the sheetrock, cut it to fit the uneven shape of the log rounds. It was not something that could be calculated or measured. It required real craftsmanship, something I sorely lacked. A few halting efforts had shown me it wouldn't come easily.

Instead, I built a drafting desk from leftover lumber and spent the last weeks of winter evenings planted there, in comfortable range of the woodstove. In half-inch scale, I churned out plans for the sundeck, one overly elaborate drawing after another in plan, elevation, and cross-section – two or three drafts of each with additional detailing on the side. Annie justified the fuss by saying that the sundeck would be the most elaborate piece of carpentry I'd ever undertaken, and I needed to get it right. Personally, I called it what it was – sloth and procrastination. But, in my defense, during vacation week that spring I hunkered down and built it, exactly as drawn. I'd designed one section of the outer rail like a bisected picnic table – a long bench and an off-set table section placed comfortably at the elbows. Four people could sit in a row, taking their meals or nursing their beverages while facing out to the forest and the beaver pond. The deck gave us comfortable, every-day access to our picture-book view and was fairly handsome of its own accord, delighting Annie and surprising me more than anyone. We christened it by dragging out a pad and every blanket in the house and sleeping under the Dipper.

Annie bribed Karl with berry pies, and he drove down his tractor and tilled the garden for us. It ran from the edge of the deck almost to the rear treeline, leaving the main yard space clear for play. I sank some posts and fenced it in for her, while she laid her crop rows out with string. She planted an ambitious mix – peas and beans and carrots and onions and potatoes – each in a single long row staked at the deck end and marked with the empty seed packet. A thicket of tomatoes filled out the rest of the fenced area. She planted the pumpkin patch outside the fence, free to swarm as it would out back.

As it turned out, she never harvested a single plant from that garden. She never saw a leaf of fall foliage from that deck. Our never-ending long weekend didn't make it through year one. The disaster that June changed everything. One day was sunrise on the deck, sundown at the firepit, and all of life in between. The next day she was gone.

Chapter 12

PONDSCAPE AT DAWN

The artist went missing from the next day's breakfast. He wasn't out hiking either. He was already at his easel, which he'd set near the beaver pond on the side of the road. Apparently he'd begun just past dawn. Blake and I watched from the deck while we picked at our plates. A car came barreling around the bend and swooped by him. Then a truck — you could almost see his palette lift in its draft.

"That doesn't look safe," I said at last. "Let's go get him some safety cones." The fact is, most times of day we saw only one or two cars an hour on our road. But our breakfast hour was when the tradesmen headed out.

"Good idea!" said Blake, though I'm not sure he knew what safety cones really were, by name or by intended function. They'd historically served us as hockey goalposts, or corner kick markers, or bicycle slalom gates. We walked up to the Parenteaus', gave a courtesy tap on the door, and borrowed the cones from their shed. Blake carried one of them down the driveway, swinging it from one side of his body to the other while calling over his shoulder to the pigs. I took his hand when we reached the road.

The artist didn't notice us until we were right on him. His surprise turned to puzzlement as we circled around and coned him in, but he said nothing and kept at his work. As we made our exit we tried to resist unauthorized glances at the canvas, but I did notice that it sat horizontally on the easel. The first two paintings had been vertical, in orientation with the great pines. Yesterday's *Garden at Noon with Figure* was horizontal, but given its narrow scope – essentially a house, lawn, and garden – I figured that the pond view in progress would qualify as the artist's first official landscape on our grounds. Blake stomped on my foot, looking to be chased back to the house. His duck-billed cap flew off as he reached the lawn, and I scooped it in stride. When we arrived panting at the porch I looked back at the artist. He'd watched us all the way back. After a moment he bent once again, like a peasant in the fields, to the lower quarter of the canvas.

"You know what else we should do? We should make him a better easel so he doesn't have to scrunch over all the time."

"Good idea!" said Blake. It was his phrase of the week.

So while the artist labored below us on the road, I sat at the deck rail and sketched out an idea for an adjustable easel. Blake worked next to me with his black crayon. For any question that an inspection of the current easel could answer, I went to the binoculars for a better look. I adjusted them then for Blake, who stared out for some time, elbows propped on the deck rail, watching the newest painting take form, one rapid-fire brushstroke after another.

I had plenty of scrap wood in the basement and was in production within the hour. With the deck rail as a sawhorse I cut the pieces to length. A door hinge served to swing the back leg of the tripod. Screws at intervals provided multiple settings for the canvas. This simple change was the big improvement over his portable easel, which had the single fixed shelf. My edition would also be a lot sturdier. The artist, now wedged in with bright orange cones, was oblivious, both to my labors and to Blake's ongoing surveillance.

The Parenteau boys dropped in and started taking turns riding Blake's Big-Wheels trike, their overlong legs bent at grotesque angles as they pedaled. Jamie went back for one of their old Big-Wheels, and with the second one in play they were soon all in the basement, running madcap loops around the central stairwell, whooping it up and peeling out on the smooth cement floor. I could hear them from the deck, and even more clearly when I went in for *Pine Trees on a Summer Morning*, which I pulled from the mantel to test the easel at its various settings. All the while, the artist labored on.

I made my adjustments and finished about noon, just as the boys emerged from the basement, flushed and soaked with sweat. The new easel was an ungainly eight feet but would accommodate a good-sized canvas at half a dozen elevations. There'd be no more scrunching or reaching.

Blake and I made sandwiches, and the five of us ate them on the porch. If the artist sensed the second meal of the day being consumed there without him, he showed no sign of it. The boys took turns with the binoculars, keeping him under steady surveillance. They reported his taking multiple tugs from the clay jug. We were waiting for the strategic moment when he'd bend into some protracted work near the bottom of the canvas.

"Bingo," said Kevin, peering through the glasses.

We jumped into action. I lugged the easel, and Blake carried the artist's sandwich in a paper bag. We approached the pond in single file, silent and unnoticed.

"Excuse me," I said at last. "The boys and I thought this might be useful."

The artist jumped out of his bent position. It was the second surprise interruption of the day, and this was a larger, more intrusive party. He stepped back, unspeaking, as I set the new easel into place. Taking huge liberties now, I lifted his work-in-progress and demonstrated how to place it at the various settings on the new easel, leaving it finally at a high setting where the low edge of the canvas was easily accessed. Blake handed him the sandwich. Koby pointed to the pond, where the dark form of a beaver skimmed at the surface.

We headed back to the house and resumed our watch. The artist was as we'd left him, standing upright, the sandwich bag in one hand, the palette in the other. At length he set the sandwich on the old easel. He gave the new easel a slight turn, dipped his brush, and, standing quite comfortably, returned to the lower quarter of the canvas.

He didn't budge for a long many hours. We checked in periodically. At some point he must have eaten the sandwich – it disappeared from view. The day passed into late afternoon, into a brilliant sunset of orange and violet, and then into that most deceiving time just after – the time that looks almost pitch when seen from inside, but is still quite viable for those out in it. Blake and I walked to the pond just then, our eyes adjusting halfway down. We could make out the artist, kneeling and rolling his brushes into sections of cloth. I called out so as not to startle him for a third time. We exchanged a few words, and then I gathered up the traffic cones and both easels, the artist his painting, and Blake the artist's bundles. The headlights of a car came into view. We waited well off the road until it passed by. Then we traipsed back to the house. The artist straggled – he looked closer to sixty than thirty there in the fading light.

As Blake held the door, I set the easels inside. The artist set the painting on the porch and stooped to remove his shoes, laboring like a much older man as Blake held steady at the door. When the artist and his painting were finally indoors I handed him a glass of water. He collapsed on the couch as Blake and I settled in for a look.

It was the most stunning piece of art I had ever seen. The plant life fronting the pond was simply splotch-work, an abstract grouping of color, shapeless, vaguely appealing in its own right, but nothing more. The same could be said of the water – horizontal dabs of black, blue-grays, and amber – amorphous, unrecognizable when viewed apart from its surroundings. But as a whole, the scene was a perfect pondscape, each element borrowing and emerging from the others. And though it was far too beautiful for this world, it was our particular pond, unmistakable and like no other. The beaver lodge broke from the water like a bale from some enchanted hayfield, below and right of center. A jagged pile, crudely fashioned, it glimmered in glorious reds and ambers, very nearly aglow, as if hosting a great torchlit council within. Leafless black specters of long-drowned trees writhed knee-deep at the water's far edge. Beyond them, others lush in summer leaf looked on from their more solid footing, smug and mildly disapproving.

Chapter 13

THE CANDLELIT MARCH

I'm surprised now at how little I remember. Blake had been napping, and I remember running to the phone so it wouldn't ring a second time. Betty was working the police dispatch that afternoon, and she was the one on the other end. I think I'd have understood more easily if it had been a stranger, an anonymous voice on the line. I remember going dark, and feeling off my balance, like I'd been hit from behind, my head driven into the glass. I remember vomiting neatly into the toilet, and thinking to brush my teeth after. And right then, as I rinsed my brush and heard Blake beginning to stir, before I really even believed what I'd heard, I saw my role, as in a vision. I'd sew up the gash in my boy's cocoon, make it whole again before he tumbled out and down onto the forest floor.

I remember quiet, tightly-structured catharses each morning: confusion at waking up in Blake's bed; realization that I'd awakened into a nightmare rather than out of one; and then wonder at the fact that either of us had slept at all. And those were generally the clearest moments of the day. I'd then enter my normal waking state, that is to say, a condition of perpetual shock. I was a full-time parenting zombie, eyes fixed forward, steering Blake through the hours. I let other people handle everything else. I wouldn't even answer their questions. You decide, I'd say. You decide.

I remember the march. A long line of kids made a candlelit walk on a starry June night, all the way from the high school. I watched them come down the road, hundreds in all, police escorts front and rear. They crossed the culvert, turned into the driveway, and, as if in some sudden inspiration of choreography, circled the great pine. I met them there for serial hugs, hundreds of them – boy-hugs, girl-hugs, group-hugs. I remember the scents of unwashed hair and the scents of a dozen shampoos. One student consulted his watch and said, "Moonrise in twenty-one minutes." Several of them mentioned that she was off to a shinier purpose. I didn't know she'd used that line in school, and I didn't have the heart to say I didn't believe a word of it.

I noticed the line of lights doubling back on itself, the first of them filing back past the last of them. Not all were students. Fellow teachers filtered past, cafeteria staff, janitors. Rita Lonborg took my hand and said, "I'm so terribly sorry." Charlie Beanland said he still remembered that roast chicken. The Parenteaus came through, all of them in Sunday dress. Even Bobby Bethune was there, kissing me on both cheeks with a look that was crazier, if possible, than when we'd bought the house. With the last of the hugs the line straightened, and I watched the tail of it twinkle down the road and disappear back into the trees. I looked to the moon, which would still be a while to clear the treeline. We'd only been at that school for a year. Annie was that kind of person.

I sleepwalked through everything else, the logistics, the food, the wellwishers, the stream of family, the service, the wave of legal stuff. Grief is not nearly as tidy as all that. We slog through events like those, and through the whole of our suddenly uprooted lives, as if watching from another room. We juggle foggy notions with chance inputs and obstructed feelings. Our brains flicker and smolder, something random takes hold. A sentence unsaid, a smattering of sorrow, a flash of anger, an odd shot of guilt. And then you let the cat out, scratch your head, make your kid his breakfast.

After a couple weeks, everything had gone quiet. Blake and I were on our own, alone in the cabin, alone on the grounds. I was learning through the haze what it meant to take care of him, as a single parent, by myself – how to pace a single hour and then another, through the bigger picture of a whole day. I felt myself disappearing, pouring myself wholly and absolutely into the charge. When he'd finally go down for his nap it was like I'd come up from under the lake, sputtering and gasping for air. Or like I'd walked through some curtain between two worlds, suddenly on the clock of my free time, frantic to make use of every second.

She'd insisted on life insurance for both of us as soon as Blake was born. I'd always been more of the money person – or, rather, she wasn't at all a money person – but she'd been way ahead of me on that one. It was typical of her that in the one single financial inspiration of her lifetime she drove the most important money decision we ever made. If I ever thought about that stuff in the weeks after the accident, it was only in flashes – but something in me never really believed the money would come. When a check actually appeared I was astounded. Can a check that big just show up in your mailbox? Could I even accept it? It seemed something like blood money, a lot of money, but compensation so feeble I wanted to refuse it on principle alone. It took me a week to come to terms with it.

When I'd finally deposited the check I picked up the phone and called Rita Lonborg. I told her I needed the year off. She sounded like a sad old grandmother – couldn't have been nicer. She said my job would be waiting for me. She asked after Blake, asked if there was anything else she could do. Just before we hung up she said that the science department was making the leaf project an annual school-wide event in Annie's memory. I didn't mention that I doubted I'd ever really be back. In my head it was just as likely that Annie'd be back as I would.

Where was she, anyway? Blake, who could barely talk at that time, was asking that question, over and over. I'd answer as best I could, and then he'd ask again, sometimes right away, sometimes a couple hours later. Sometimes I'd just say, I don't know. And the fact is, I didn't. I was asking myself the same thing, over and over, just like he was. I remember thinking about the stick figure family decals on the truck – what was I supposed to do now, scrape her off?

Her clothes, her gear, her things were all over the house. I thought for the longest time about what to do with it. I was going to gather it all up, give it away, throw it away. But I kept putting it off, and in the end I just couldn't get rid of it. She really liked some of that stuff. I couldn't leave it all over the place either – I didn't need reminders in those few moments when I wasn't already thinking about her. So I packed it all in a closet – her shoes, her clothes, her papers, her bathroom things. Out of view, but available, right where we could find them if they were ever needed, whatever that meant.

After a while I couldn't look at her pictures, but I never took them down either. I knew perfectly well where every single one of them was displayed around the house, where and when they'd been taken, how she'd been positioned, what she'd been wearing. I knew every time I walked by one, just as if I'd looked. All day long I'd swallow things I'd think to say to her – it had been as natural as breathing – normal mundane things, stupid jokes, catchwords we had. At night though, when Blake was in bed and sleeping, I'd let myself talk to her, in a kind of half voice, running through the events of the day like she was off on some trip and we were on speakerphone. I could read to Blake, but try as I did, I couldn't read a book by myself any more. I was absolutely incapable of it. I even tried to read aloud, but that was even worse, the stunt of a lugubrious clown.

I hadn't touched any of the building materials for more than a year. Dust lay thick on the sheetrock stack at the top of the stairs. I must have stepped around that pile a couple thousand times on the way to and from the bed, to and from the bathroom. As a single parent I didn't have much time to work, even without a real job. Blake was either awake and needed looking after, or he was asleep and needed something resembling quiet. But sleep deprivation, apathy, way too much beer, constant fatigue – these were my real problems. Cases of empties piled in the basement. I always rinsed and repacked them neatly, stacking them as a tribute to something I couldn't quite name. Blake had been sleeping downstairs so long it had become as natural as a beaver tucked in its lodge. Neither of us could remember any other arrangement. It was hard to believe he'd started there in a crib. If it had been a project I knew I could handle I may have made a run at it. But scribing that sheetrock was going to drive me crazy – I knew it. And I knew enough to avoid things that might set me off.

PART TWO

Chapter 14

THE GALLERY

I was admiring sunset colors more suited to a hallucination than to this earth when I realized that the artist had been with us nearly a week. In that run of days we'd all settled into our patterns. Blake was an early riser, but more often than not the artist was gone by the time we'd surface – he'd be miles into his morning ambulations, his tent neatly folded on the porch. Early in the week I'd told him he didn't have to take his tent down every morning. But he'd kept right on with it, leaving it folded and tucked neatly against the house. At first that made me think each day might be his last, but now I thought nothing of it.

He'd shown a pattern of painting certain scenes twice, once with the light of early morning, and again with the light of late afternoon. Paintings in morning light he'd complete in a single day, cutting his morning walks short and walking again in the evenings. Paintings in afternoon light would carry over to be completed the next day. Those two days accommodated longer morning walks. Blake and I tended to drag out our breakfast preparations on those days, stalling for his return. As the week went on, he seemed to return more promptly. Besides breakfast, the three of us would share the occasional lunch – though more often Blake and I would deliver him a sandwich at his post – and most of our evening meals on the deck. Those meals were our primary times together. Like Blake, the artist tended to retire shortly after dark. For the most part we didn't disturb him at his work, and he hardly ever came into the house, though I made it clear he was welcome. Any other position would have been ludicrous. Our formerly spartan living room had become something out of the Louvre on his account.

Already, we were up to four paintings in there. Blake and I had begun to call it "the Gallery." The mantel had been quickly overwhelmed with the two portraits of the pines. They were a wild explosion of color, rogue flora blooming and bursting from their pedestrian planters. I hadn't really wanted to pound a nail into the wall for *Garden at Noon with Figure* – it seemed presumptuous on my part – so I built a makeshift easel and placed it where the light was best in the corner. But when the fourth one had come in – *Pondscape at Dawn* – it absolutely screamed for the central space over the couch, opposite the mantel. I pondered it all day, through the quiet morning and into the afternoon, when the artist began his second pondscape. At dusk we helped him carry up his things, and when he went for his dip in the lake, I pounded the nail, and I hung it.

Blake and I set the fire in the pit. We liked that routine, the single piece of crumbled newspaper in a bed of dried pine cones, the teepee of long twigs over that, the log cabin of sticks around that, another teepee, another cabin, each with successively larger pieces. It was getting late, and we were hungry. But we wanted the artist on hand for the ceremonial lighting. We sat around the unlit fire. I whittled sticks for cooking skewers and handed them to Blake, who liked to whip them around like swords. Just as we'd about given up, the dark figure of the artist emerged from the even darker forest, still toweling his face and head. Blake ran to him, a wraithling in the fading light.

"Mister Willem, we're about to light the fire."

The flame on the extra-long match showed brightly, feeble and flickering though it was, as I fed it through the teepee and cabin maze.

It touched the wadded paper and flared, exploded on the cones, then began to leap from structure to structure. Soon it crackled nearly waist high. We shifted back on our stoops, away from the sudden heat, each of us cast in a glow of orange.

As soothing as I find campfires to be, I'm never really at rest with them. I'm constantly in pursuit of the optimal burn, standing every minute or so to reach for a new piece of wood, or to shift a piece that's already burning, to lure the flame into an area of void. I want a clean bed of ashes in the morning, not charred chunks left to sit and go oily in the rains. The artist for his part was more interested in the stars, which had popped out rather dramatically. He spent minutes at a time staring up, his neck craning at unnatural angles until I handed him his sausage skewer and we began to cook. Blake held long sticks into the flame until their ends caught fire. He could do that for hours.

The teepees and cabins bowed and collapsed as we ate. Big chunks of the fire retreated into heaps of seething coals, and the shadows around it grew deep. The artist had no knowledge of marshmallows, so I showed him how to find the pockets of cooking heat, low and out of any flame, toasting him a perfect golden-brown introduction. He took to it, and within minutes, sugary strings hung off his beard like starter webs.

Before bed, Blake insisted that the artist come in to have a look at *Pondscape at Dawn* on the wall. As always, the artist removed his shoes, but not his straw hat, before entering. He stood quietly, rubbing his chin and staring at the painting as if seeing it for the first time. I had a surprise for both of them, which I now pulled from behind a chair and held up to the wall. The framed effect was pleasing. I'd pressed the glass to minimize the folds, and the one light food smudge, in my opinion, added character and authenticity. Blake grasped it at once. "The beaver napkin!" he said. "Great idea!"

The artist bowed. "It is a great honor," he said. Blake bowed right back at him. I noticed then that Blake was in stocking feet, with his hat still on, just like the artist. I tapped a nail in the wall and performed the ceremonial hanging of the frame. The artist seemed genuinely moved, perhaps a bit confused. He began a snail's-paced tour through the whole collection, studying each piece at great length, lingering like a paying customer. I could picture him with a satchel and museum-issue headphones, taking notes, avoiding eye contact with security personnel, ignoring announcements to please clear the Gallery.

After some time, Blake and I set into our pre-bed routine. The artist was no longer looking at paintings, but still he hovered, to the point where things became a little awkward. He picked up our pin art box and flipped it several times. The silver pins rattled louder than I ever could have imagined – not at all a noise I welcomed at bedtime. He imprinted his hand, and then his fist, and then, incredibly, I saw him shove his whole face into the grid. Blake and I settled into the easy chair, his tiny hips wedged in the corner, his pajama-clad legs stretched straight out. I pulled out a book. The artist didn't excuse himself, but, with a final crash, he tossed the pin art box onto the couch, and then sat there himself. Blake and I both stared at him, and he stared right back, as if expecting something. I couldn't think of anything else to do, so I began to read.

You may recall the story. Mike Mulligan operates an antiquated steam shovel that goes by the decidedly non-industrial name of Mary Anne. Mary Anne doesn't talk – her mouth is generally full of dirt – but she does have eyes in her dipper, giving her a pleasing impression something in the manner of a friendly dinosaur. The two face heavy competition from newer diesel-powered shovels and flee to the country to find work. There they find themselves against a heavy deadline – they must dig a foundation in a single day. They work furiously, perhaps even heroically, and finish just in time. But they've forgotten to leave a ramp, a way out for Mary Anne.

I took a quick look at the artist just as Mary Anne found herself trapped in the terminal corner. His jaws were flexed in consternation. What would become of the digging duo? When it was resolved that she would become a furnace in the building, and Mike the pipe-smoking janitor, he exhaled audibly and sank deeper into his seat.

Blake and I had read that book at least a dozen times, and now for the first time since the earliest readings, he asked a question. "Did Mary Anne want to be a furnace?"

"Well, I've always wondered about that myself," I answered. "But they seem pretty happy in that last picture, don't they?"

"What do you think, Mister Willem?" Blake asked, walking over and handing the book to our guest. The artist took a long look.

"Yes, they look happy in this picture." And then, after a pause, as if he couldn't help himself: "But I think she's meant to be a steam shovel, working outdoors."

"Me too," said Blake. He crawled onto his mattress in the corner. He settled for a moment, and then in a sleepy voice he said, "Good night, Mister Willem."

"Good night, Master Blake." And with that, the artist headed out to his tent.

Chapter 15

NIGHTSPLITTING

From very early on I'd had no faith in the rural police. Lieutenant Samford was adept enough at mapping out the incident – the point of collision, the angle of impact, the points of recovery. He worked out the speed of the vehicle, and even gleaned something about the vehicle itself – a truck, or a car with a high set grill. But after some days his approach began to feel like a hypothetical exercise, an end in itself. He seemed to consider building the elaborate impact model as his entire scope of work, as if someone else would take it from there. But, of course, in our little town there was no one else to do that. In contrast to his meticulous approach to the model, Lieutenant Samford had no strategy, and very little interest, it seemed, in finding the driver. I didn't have the slightest hope that he'd solve anything. And the fact is, I didn't need it. My thought from the beginning was to find the driver myself. I had vague notions as to how I'd actually find him, and even vaguer notions of what I'd do if I did. Whoever was driving that car had hit my wife, a woman on a bicycle, at somewhere near sixty miles an hour – and never even slowed down.

The way I figured, it was a local road, so chances were it was a local car. A couple times a week I'd ask the Parenteaus to watch Blake, and I'd head out on foot. These were not charming little nature hikes, but long grim treks along the roads, miles and miles through scattered clusters of sad-looking rural homes. The cat would follow along, not like a dog in stride at my heels, but in the way of cats, darting in and out of view, walking on walls, disappearing for long stretches and then checking back in. There were pockets of happy-looking homes, with flowers and bird-feeders and well-tended lawns and gardens. But most were ill-conceived, hideous-looking places ringed with cinderblock garages, dogs in chain-swept circles of dirt, tree stumps and scabby trees still standing, stone-pocked yards, plastic sheds. These were not the homes of people who lived in the woods out of any particular fondness for them. I had the feeling on those walks that most of them would have burnt down the whole forest for fifteen grand.

The Bethunes had settled in one such place, a cramped and charmless downgrade, its tiny yard already filling with refuse. But I was in no mood for empathy. I was seething, and on the hunt, scanning and cataloguing every vehicle I came across, looking for a certain damage pattern on the front right quarter. I walked up people's driveways and circled their vehicles. When the occasional dog would charge I'd chase it back where it came from, at full sprint, with a soundless ferocity it couldn't have expected in a passer-by. If somebody came through the house door I'd just walk away. Like some lunatic country meter maid, I noted every single car in my pocket-sized pad – address, plate number, make, model, color, and, of course, scratches, dents, obvious repairs. If I thought a car was shut up in a garage I'd note that too and try to see it later.

Physical exhaustion, I suppose, was as much the objective as cataloguing the cars. As I went through the closest clusters of homes and began to build my endurance, I took to longer walks, crossing the state line to neighborhoods almost large enough to be towns. Some days I was gone six, seven hours at a time. The cat stopped following. I don't remember thinking about much of anything.

I turned down any invitation I got. When I wasn't parenting I was walking. Just not ready, I'd say. I had very little interaction with any adults – a chat in the driveway with Karl or Betty, a sentence or two with a store clerk. Clare and my friends in the city were pushing me to bring Blake back in, and sometimes I'd think maybe that would be best. I had an unfinished feeling at the thought of leaving, but maybe the isolation wasn't good for either of us. More exposure to people, more bustle, a little more support – it might all make sense. But then I'd see Blake running in the yard, playing in the leaves, chasing the cat, feeding the pigs. I'd feel the colors of the sunset and the creaking of the trees. And then I'd think otherwise. The quiet, the long slow days in our little slice of the forest – in daylight it seemed like the only path.

At night, on the other hand, I was completely losing it. I'd drink on the deck, four or five quick beers, planted in the rocker, watching the stars. And then most nights, I'd tromp down to the woodpiles. There was endless stock to be split for the stove, staggeringly heavy bark-wrapped blocks of pine, two feet thick or more, in piles higher than my shoulder. And there, just beside, was the maul, set in the chopping block, its sap-stained handle angled up in a perpetual summons. In daylight the split pine shone bright, almost blonde, and gave off a thick foresty perfume. But in darkness and the cool of night all that was lost. It was pounding for pounding's sake; a shapeless, odorless line of wooden dead weights; an unending string of rough-hewn challengers.

Floating on my beer buzz, I'd set the kerosene lantern on a stack of blocks and crank it to its brightest setting. It threw just enough light so I could make out the grain in the wood and set my target at the center of the concentric circles. In my mind I could put that maul within half an inch. The reality is, it's a wonder I still have both feet. These were full-windup, long-arching, gut-grunting swings, wrists snapping for extra speed at the weighted head, always looking for the single clean split, through the log and on into the chopping block. Some sections I would split into quarters. The larger ones I'd split into sixes or eights, leaving them neat on the block, like vertical pizza. White pine is full of knots — sometimes the maul head would simply bounce. I'd turn the log thirty degrees, or flip it over, but I'd never give in, hacking away, pouring sweat, swearing like a sailor, guzzling beer at every small triumph. Sometimes the knotty bits would be unrecognizable as firewood, pounded into gnarly chunks but chucked into the same pile with the clean-split lengths. It would all burn.

The first night of the artist's stay I figured there'd be no woodsplitting, not while he was camped there in the yard. I sat in the rocker, my arms and shoulders bristling for their workout, and drank eight beers. On the second night, as I settled back into the rocker, a light showed within his tent. It was not a lantern like mine, but something more like a real flame, a candle perhaps. At just that moment he must have snuffed it; the tent plunged into darkness. I could still see its outline, or was it an illusion, a lingering optical imprint? Somehow I took it as a communal cue, an unspoken imperative to shut it down, to call it a night. I finished the beer I'd started, my first, stood up and rinsed the can. And, instead of opening another, I checked in on Blake, turned and walked up the stairs. I stepped around the sheetrock pile, cleaned myself up, and went to bed. Rest didn't come easily. I did some pushups, got back into bed, got up and did some more. Jumpy and distracted, even in exhaustion, I slogged through a few dismal hours. But in time I slept.

Chapter 16

THE SWORD IN THE STONE

Something about the artist must have changed my outlook. If a complete unknown could wander up our road, pitch a tent, and paint like a god, then surely I could sketch out a couple of logs and finish the work upstairs. The construction timeline had become an embarrassment, making me the perfect example of the guy I never wanted to be, the after-hours do-it-yourselfer hitting the wall and turning his house into a perpetual eyesore of unfinished work. When Blake was sleeping soundly, I strapped on the tool-belt, bubbling with sudden optimism.

I held a two-foot strip of sheetrock in my left hand, a number two pencil in my right. I picked one log, studied it, drew it. Then another, and another – three logs, each of them uniquely shaped, to each strip of sheetrock. I set the strip on a work surface and cut along the pattern with a blade, scribing through the papery surface and deep into the chalk. I pulled away the cut and slid the scribed remainder into the grooves of the logs. It stuck in some places and flared out hideously in others.

I penciled on some adjustments and cut it again. Again, I wedged it into the grooves. Again, not even close. I hadn't really matched any of the three logs in question. None of this was a particular surprise. Why should things suddenly have been different? Looking back now, the only real surprise was how long I stayed at it – sketches, cuts, lousy fits, expletives. The sheetrock strip narrowed with every cut. After five or six cuts, it'd be too short to span the studs, and I'd have to start on a new one. There was no reason to believe that the next piece would be better than the last, or than any of my attempts many months earlier. But I kept grimly on, like a compulsive gambler throwing himself to ruin, floundering through a half dozen pieces, none of them with the slightest chance of success. I threw the last one into the wall, and it exploded more loudly than I'd expected. I held my breath and listened, watching the little cloud of sheetrock dust as it settled to the floor. There was no sound from Blake. He was still asleep. The fact is, if he hadn't been sleeping down there I'd have been screaming like a lunatic.

Instead, I was seething quietly at the window, staring out at the patch of light it threw into the yard. And there, centered directly in that patch, stood the artist, hands on his hips, staring right back at me. Almost before I could process this, he turned and left the light. A few moments later I heard the front door open and close, quietly, and heard him climbing the stairs. He resumed the same position at the top of the steps, hands on hips, assessing the project, without a word. He was wearing a jacket I hadn't seen before, an odd number with no collar and a large single button at the neck.

"Hey, you've got your shoes on," I said.

It was the first time I'd seen them in the house. He ignored the comment. He stood motionless, still studying the situation – the partition wall dying into the logs, and the discarded sheetrock segments cut into log-like rounds and piled sadly on the floor. He grabbed a fresh sheetrock strip – I'd pre-cut dozens of them – and tossed his jacket to the floor.

"Give me the pencil."

Tucking the sheetrock strip into his left elbow, he knelt, studied the logs and drew a few quick sweeping curves, doctoring each just slightly before handing the strip back to me.

"Cut this."

I made the cut and handed it back. He slid it into the slots. The fit was perfect. I bent in for a closer look – there was no more than an eighth-inch gap anywhere along the curve of the logs – on the very first try. I thought, strangely, of the boy Arthur pulling the sword from the stone, and then, stranger still, of Cinderella sliding into her slipper. Astounded and nearly drunk with elation, I pushed the artist playfully to one side, and screwed in the form-fitted segment. After months of frustration, the answer had simply strolled in from the woods. We worked from the floor to eight feet, piece by piece, then shifted to the next section of wall. I was drawing and holstering my screwgun like a six-shooter, saying giddy things like, "We're really coming along now!" and "Nice cut there, Willem!" The artist was obviously in no such mood. He didn't respond to any of my inanities, but I kept right on, not really knowing why. The rain set back in. It was an hour or so before he said a word:

"Does Master Blake have only the single striped shirt?"

"I was going to ask the same thing about you. Seems like I'm the only guy around here who ever changes his clothes."

I regretted saying it. I'd been surprised by the question, and had answered without thinking. He didn't respond, and it was clear he saw no humor in it.

"It's good to travel light," I said by way of an apology. "Blake wears the shirt by choice. It's a particular favorite. We're going on two months with it."

We fell back into the quiet rhythm of the work. The night was so dark the windows were like mirrors but for the trickles of rainwater. I saw that his mood had sunk again. He stared darkly from under his farmer's hat into the black running windows. Was it the beads of water or his own reflection that had his attention?

He asked then: "Does Master Blake have no mother?"

"Killed on her bicycle a year ago June."

Silence.

"I'm sorry to hear."

"Thank you."

Silence.

"The woman in the pictures?"

"Yes."

Silence.

"Is that the cause of his beating the copperware in the morning?"

"I didn't know you'd heard that. I thought you were always gone on your walks."

"I often set out at the gongs."

"You haven't heard the least of it," I said, thinking of the nocturnal woodsplitting.

Silence again. I realized I hadn't answered his question.

"I don't know why he beats the pans," I said. "I never thought of it like that."

I thought about it now as we worked through another section. Was the pot-beating an instinctive and self-administered exorcism, a casting out of the anger and the sadness at the beginning of the day? Or was it, as I'd thought, just something he liked to do, a warm-up for the day? Were those essentially the same concepts presented in a different light? And which was the proper light, anyway? Would I worry and fret and follow the counsel of professionals? Or would I just be his friend and his teacher and set him up as best I could in the world that was presented to him, a forest creature making do. I thought of him in shorts, walking on the road, with his skinny little legs and his clunky white sneakers. I thought of him climbing into the canoe, in his little red water shoes, stepping over the thwarts, taking his spot in the galley.

The artist and I were in autopilot mode just then, lost in the rhythm of the work. Each of us contributed his skill in turn, an unspeaking two-man machine, passing pieces hand to hand for marking, cutting, and setting. At each small milestone of progress we grabbed another stack of pre-cut sheetrock sections, working ourselves steadily through the plan. In less than two hours we'd completed the circuit – both sides of every partition wall, at the log edges from the floor to the ceiling joists at eight feet. That's where the Bethunes had roofed in the bedrooms. My plans were more ambitious. They called for cathedral ceilings, open to the ridge beam, but that would require scaffolding. I suggested we call it a night.

We washed up downstairs. I put out some cold chicken and offered beer, juice, or water, and then as an afterthought, milk. Surprisingly, he chose the latter. I joined him in the first glass of cold milk in as long as I could remember. And by the way he devoured it, the artist had what might have been the first midnight chicken in as long as he could remember.

"What did you mean by plate numbers?" he asked at the end of the meal.

So he HAD heard. It was just like the artist to pick up a conversation from two days earlier, nearly mid-sentence, as if no time had passed at all.

"I used to trek around the neighborhood – well, around a lot of neighborhoods really. I was looking for cars that might have had certain markings on them."

"And you kept track of the cars in the book."

"Yes."

"And how to know what kind of markings?"

"Well, I sort of reproduced the accident." And then I told him how I'd driven to the site and set my own bicycle on the side of the road, right where she'd been hit. I told him that to make her weight I'd piled sandbags over the seat, a hundred and twenty pounds of them. I told him I'd assumed fifteen miles an hour for her and subtracted that from the sixty the police had estimated for the car or truck. I'd backed the truck a quarter mile down the road, gunned it to forty-five, taken the angle, and plowed right in. The bike had crunched under the truck, and I'd watched it skitter away in the mirror. I'd stopped, and everything was still for a minute. A couple swipes of the wipers more or less cleared the sand from the windshield. And then I turned around and headed home.

We sat quietly for a minute or two.

"Do you want to sleep inside? It's raining like hell, and I have a pad you could put on the floor."

"No, but thank you. I will make my camp." He stood and put his plate on the counter and his hat on his head. "Tomorrow will bring good light," he said with something approximating a smile, and shut the door softly behind him.

Chapter 17

LONG-LEGGED GUESTS

From the way the sun slanted in I knew it was the latest I'd slept in years. It may have been the best I'd felt, physically, in many months, after a run of alcohol-free nights and now a long late sleep. But where was Blake?

I ran down the stairs. His bed was empty. The kitchen was empty. But there through the window I saw them, Blake and the artist, seated at the deck rail, their backs to me, their faces to the sun. I walked out to join them. Blinded at first in the brilliance of the morning, I saw at last that they were working with crayons.

I'd always been loyal to Crayola, to the iconic yellow and green box. I'd bought Blake the small sets first, the eight-pack, and then the twenty-four pack, leaving him room to grow as he advanced. The bigger sets made no sense, since he drew almost exclusively in black, working it to the nub until I pulled back the paper for him. But on his fourth birthday I couldn't hold out any longer, and I bought him his first big-boy sixty-four box, complete with built-in sharpener. I'd hoped the sixty-four box would astound him with choice and move him into the spectrum, but it hadn't quite panned out – the built-in sharpener was seeing heavy activity in black, while the other crayons were still pristine in their points. Whenever I began to think this a little strange I just had to reflect on my own color obsessions at his age – burnt sienna and raw umber. I think Blake was more interested in the design of the box than anything else. He loved dumping out all the crayons and pulling out the four cardboard mini-cartons, each configured for two rows of eight, then packing them back on their cardboard shelves and reloading all sixty-four crayons, points up.

The artist had dumped out all the crayons too, but he'd laid them out side-by-side in a perfect spectrum – reds bleeding into oranges, and then into yellows, greens, blues and purples. The blacks, grays and browns he'd arranged separately. He and Blake were playing a game. The artist would call out a subject from the view off the deck – "the grass in the lawn," or "the leaves in that tree." Blake would answer, "Good idea!" and then they'd take turns pulling crayons for the colors they saw in the grass or the leaves. Blake did open every round with black, but he engaged in the color exercise from there, smearing samples on the tablet set before him. The artist would follow on, consolidating Blake's squiggles and smudges, filling the spaces, and, as if through some sort of sorcery, producing color studies that were remarkably persuasive. Then Blake would make a suggestion of his own, like "your shoes!" or "the side of the house!" and they'd be at it for another round. The artist would write block letter titles over each color study – GRASS, LEAVES, HOUSE, SHOES. His hands were steadily at work, seeming to think on their own, as he magicked Blake's smudges, printed the titles, freed up new pages, and replaced the crayons properly within the spectrum, all while maintaining a calm but steady banter.

"Your hair!" Blake called out, and the artist whipped off his hat and called dramatically for a mirror. He settled in short order for a spoon, angling it over his head and gaping while Blake laughed and each of them reached for golds and oranges and browns. Feeling a little left out, I grabbed a book and settled onto the daybed. Before I knew it I'd actually read ten pages. Blake announced that they were headed up to feed the pigs. I ran inside to get them the slop bucket – we saved all our food scraps for just that purpose – and settled back onto the daybed. By the time they got back I'd read ten more.

The artist set up once more by the pond. I was pleased that he seemed to prefer his new easel. Once more Blake and I set the cones around him and left him at his work. At noon we took him his sandwich and lemonade. He seemed less disoriented at the interruption than usual, and something was rustling in the brush to the left of the pond – so we lingered and listened. "A beaver?" I whispered. It was difficult not to steal a look at the canvas while we waited, but the rules were more than clear, well established through the artist's prior applications of grunts and scowls. We kept our eyes on the underbrush. The rustling went silent for a moment, and then we heard it again – closer this time, no longer a rustle, but a crashing.

"That must be some beaver," I said softly. No one seemed to appreciate the humor. "Maybe they're dropping bigger trees these days." Still no laughs. And then a massive rack of horns split the brush, and out stepped a gigantic bull moose, right onto the road, not fifteen feet from where we stood. I wouldn't have been more surprised to see a Brontosaurus. The beast was six or seven feet at the shoulders, nine or ten with the antlers all in. And I can say now on some authority, it's hard to exclude the antlers when contemplating a bull moose, particularly at close quarters. He turned to face us. I didn't make out much of an expression – a slight twitch of the nostril, a flick of the ear. But he'd tilted his head down a bit, which had the effect of bringing the horns slightly forward. I took one step back, and Blake stepped behind me. The artist was facing the moose with his back to us, a cave child before a rogue mammoth. With the non-palette hand he removed his hat, as one might before a deity. But that was his only concession – he made no defensive motion whatsoever. Behind the bull now came the cow, and a calf that was already as tall as I was. They crossed the road, passing right between our safety cones while the bull stood sentry. Their legs were so long, and their movements so gangly, that it seemed more like low speed animation than real animals passing before us. And then they were gone, plunging into the brush on the other side.

We all stood dumfounded. I noticed that the artist had a bald spot the size of a quarter. He replaced his hat and turned back our way. Blake said, "Whoa," in a half-whisper, looked at each of us, and ran off to tell the Parenteaus.

"It is a great privilege to commune with such beasts," said the artist. And with a puff of his pipe he turned back to the canvas, as if the whole thing had never happened. I walked back to the house, narrating the story for Annie, not quite aloud, but at something more than a whisper. A good story to tell could do that. Neither of us had ever seen a moose, but I'm sure she would have known to call those things "palmate antlers".

With Blake up the driveway and the artist at work, I had the inclination for a mid-day beer buzz, but then sheetrocking came to mind. With the scribing complete to eight feet, the easiest part of the whole job was right in front of me. All I had to do was set the sheets upright on the floor and screw them in. I needed a straight cut here, a cutout for a light switch or an outlet there, but the work was more or less straightforward. And, like mowing the lawn, it was visually rewarding, progress easily reviewed and admired. I checked in on Blake after an hour, but Betty was pleased to have him – "He's having his happy effect on the boys," she said. "We'll keep him for dinner."

I finished sometime near dark. The stack was reduced by half, and the upstairs looked like a whole new place. The longstanding skeleton of studs and running wire had been clad, tidy and bright to eight feet. I walked up the driveway to get Blake, and after a chat with the Parenteaus, he and I went down to the pond to check on the artist. The easel was gone, as was the artist – probably headed for his evening swim

— so we headed inside for the night. We swapped moose stories, and I gave him a tour of the sheetrock installation. It was after the bath, after pajamas, when we'd finally settled in for stories, that we noticed the painting. It sat on the artist's old easel, in the corner opposite *Garden at Noon*. He'd brought it in himself — presumably while I was up the driveway. I wondered if that timing was a coincidence, or if he'd waited for the empty house.

I might have guessed the name he'd assign it — *Pondscape in the Afternoon*. But I could never have anticipated the painting itself. The easel, by design or by chance, was perfectly aligned from the vantage point of the bed. I'd already opened the book, but we never read the first word. Before us was the story of our day, set for all time, in a code only we would ever understand. The trees stood tall and in angled reflections on the pond, lanky, long and dark, bent and knobbly, like the legs of great beasts flittering in the shadows. There was movement in them, ripples, quivers — they all but ambled off the canvas. Blake turned my attention to the sea of leaves, and their mirror on the water, where thousands of points of floating purples and glistening greens hinted at great horny creatures rising from the depths, dissolving themselves and forming once again. Further to the center and free of the trees, the water stole its pigments from a mottled sky, stretching and bending each segment like thousands of sheeny spoons. Near the beaver lodge it rippled away as if in deference or veneration, miming that rough-hewn temple in both color and shape. On the left bank, where the shadows didn't reach, reeds and pond grass stood in golden multitudes, onlookers and idolaters all. The cat leapt onto the bed, walked in tight circles, and settled. I closed the book. They were both purring, off into night's long sleep.

Chapter 18

THE CAROTENE CAT

The artist stepped inside just before breakfast. Ignoring my good mornings and my praise for the pondscape he'd left the prior night, he pulled *Pine Trees on a Summer Morning* from the mantel and lugged it straight out the door. I finished my cup and followed him out. He could do what he wanted with his paintings, though I was quite attached to all of them. But *Pine Trees on a Summer Morning* — that one was mine. I found him kneeling and prying with an awl at the back of it. He was pulling off the canvas!

"Willem, what are you doing?"

"I require canvas."

"What?"

"I've spent the last clean canvas. Next I paint on backsides. This one is the most dry."

"No, no, no. You can't paint on the backsides. We'll get you more canvas."

"I must work now. The light is very good."

"Alright then, we'll go today." He looked me right in the eye, then turned back and resumed his prying. "Willem, I'm serious. Stop doing that. We'll go right now. I'll get Blake ready. Tack that thing back on."

From that moment on, all life was on hold. Everything in his manner confirmed it. There were no concessions along the line of "Would this afternoon be more convenient?" In exchange for not mucking up the painting he'd already given us, he demanded prompt and absolute servitude. Never mind that he'd waited until the very end – it wasn't a case of running low and making measured and rational plans to resupply. Never mind that I had a four-year-old to take care of, or that I had no idea if there was a single art store within an hour's drive – canvas was the only and immediate priority.

Irritating as this was on one level, I didn't need a lot of convincing on the point. You'd have to be out of your mind to flip over one of those paintings and paint on the backside. As I saw it, he'd basically be ruining two fantastic paintings at once. But any delay, any lost day, was a lost masterpiece, at least while he was on a streak like this one. Was he always this prolific? At any rate, I couldn't imagine anything more ridiculous than this man wanting for supplies, at any time, for even an hour. I thought for a moment we might piggyback a grocery run on the errand, but realized at once that we didn't dare take the time. He was already losing good light.

I looked it up and was pleasantly surprised to find an art store just a couple exits down the highway. I shifted Blake's car seat to the middle, and without delay and for the first time ever, the three of us piled into the truck. I prompted the artist to fasten his seatbelt, and we were off, headed down our familiar road, over the culvert, past the beaver pond and bearing right to circle around the lake.

I don't know if he was distressed about losing the early light, or if he was always like this in cars, or had never actually been in a car, but from the first bend in the road he was an absolute lunatic. He started by pressing his head to the window. I could see by the strain in his back and neck that he was actually pushing hard, as if he were trying to pass his head through the glass. When he turned back my way I noticed a big white compression spot on his forehead.

"You OK, Willem?"

He ignored the question. I saw that he was sizing up my window, which was halfway down. It seemed to click with him that he could roll his own down, and he grabbed the crank and worked it almost frantically to the bottom. As we pulled onto the busier road, he lifted off the seat and leaned way out into the breeze, as if he were trying to see around the car in front of us. One freckled hand clamped his hat in place.

"Willem, what are you doing?" I realized it was the second time I'd asked him that in a very brief span.

He didn't seem to hear me out there. I realized I hadn't really considered how the artist might act in public. Here he was, in our truck, like part of the family, and suddenly he'd gone sub-human. He'd become a dog on a drive, its ears blown back, strands of drool breaking off in foamy globs. Passers-by looked at us like we were on fire. I should have pulled over, but I thought that he'd tire and sit back down, that he could only hold that position for a short while. I was sadly mistaken.

If there was any place to pull in with a red-bearded maniac leaning out your window, that place had to be the Twin City Plaza. Hideous storefronts flanked a huge field of concrete. Chunks of broken curb, battered by last winter's snowplows, lay at its edges, mangled rebar protruding at the fractures. Wax-paper wrappers and Styrofoam burger boxes, the tumbleweed of the fast food age, drifted across the painted lines. As we left the truck I gave the artist a once-over to make sure he hadn't had some sort of seizure. By the looks of him, I was more shaken than he was. He seemed very nearly like a normal person – except for the fact that he looked straight up in the air during our entire walk across the lot. Without that sixth sense he would have walked into any number of cars. I looked up too, just to see what was so interesting, and I'd have knocked into a car myself if Blake hadn't steered me clear. Cumulus clouds were running hard against a rich blue backdrop. Behind them a puffy vertical stack drifted up and up, higher than I'd have thought clouds could go, like a great waterfall I'd come across on some dreamed-up mountainous woodland trek. And then we were inside.

Given its extremely uninspiring setting, it was a good enough art store, or so I gathered from the artist's initial reaction. He didn't exactly relax – rather he seemed to gird himself for duty – but the edge of panic seemed to drop off him. Blake and I had no experience in this kind of shop, with shelves and shelves of brushes and paints, boxed sets, bottles and jars and tubes of paints of all types – oils, acrylics, watercolors. Each paint type was offered in stick form as well, endless sets of pencils and pigment sticks.

"It seems that anything you can do with a brush you can do with a stick," I said.

"Quite to the contrary," he hissed. "Nothing like the brush can be done with a stick." I quite enjoyed his haughtiness from time to time.

We waded through a small forest of papers, tablets and boards. In the section with the drawing tables and the easels, I compared the professional designs to my own. Canvas, I saw, came in many forms, pre-stretched, rolled or folded, linen or cotton, primed or unprimed. I consider myself a bit of a tool and hardware buff, but here was a whole range of specialized hardware completely unfamiliar to me – wide-mouthed canvas-stretching pliers, painting knives, canvas scrapers and shears.

The artist was all business, picking up a few tubes of paint, some solvents, a few paper tablets and, of course, a large roll of canvas. He seemed most inclined to linger in the brush section, and we made him explain the many shapes – fan, filbert, and flat, to name a few. He preferred the natural brushes to the synthetic, carrying on about the relative benefits of squirrel, goat, ox, pony, badger, hog, sable. Only when we reached the register did I realize, to my amazement, that he'd picked up a set of oil pastel sticks, and a thick pack of construction paper, in black. "For the child," he said with a sheepish half-smile. I was shocked and touched that he was buying things for Blake. He produced a small cluster of crumpled bills, but I insisted on paying. It was the least I could do. I regretted my earlier embarrassment in the truck and didn't try to stop him when he leaned back out on the way home. Blake even held his hat. The rushing air plastered his red hair straight back. I met the looks of many a gawker with what I hoped was a winning smile.

The cat was sleeping on a deck chair when we got home. Blake, as he often did, sat in front of her, staring until she woke up. The artist began to watch the cat then too. He reached for one of his new tablets and began to sketch. The cat stretched itself awake. The artist flipped a few pages and continued to draw. The cat sat tall and straight, studying him right back, trying to determine just what this strange human was about. The artist caught this pose perfectly, the cat looking straight on, its tail to the side and curled slightly upwards. One minute he's desperate enough to paint on a backside, I thought. We skip the groceries and sprint back so he can sketch the cat? Or was the good light well past?

"Come, Master Blake, if your father approves we will work with the new colors."

The two of them moved to the bench, facing out. On a piece of the black construction paper, the artist reproduced the cat sketch in a few quick strokes. "Now, Master Blake, which of yesterday's palettes shall we use to color our cat? HOUSE? GRASS? HAIR?"

"HAIR!" said Blake. And so our first finished cat shared its coloration with the artist — a carotene cat, if you will. The black pastel, as Blake quickly discovered, was pointless on the black paper. He started in with colors, as if it were perfectly natural to him. He could barely keep his squiggles within the lines, but he had a knack for great calico curls, which he spread liberally through the cat's splendid coat. The artist showed Blake the magical nature of the oil pastel sticks. Unlike crayons, they covered each other perfectly. Any mistake could be remedied, any late inspiration embraced.

Chapter 19

A RUDE INTERRUPTION

The Parenteau boys dropped by sometime after lunch, and at Blake's urging each of them produced a colorized cat of his own. Koby, at first, was reluctant to color with younger boys, especially in the open setting out there on the deck, where he might be seen. The artist recognized this at once and set about making the task seem a bit more distinguished. And so it was that we came by his own *Cat*, the only one he ever painted among the dozens whose outlines he sketched as templates for the boys. It was also the only time I ever saw him play overtly to an audience. We were all huddled around him, and as fast as I'd seen him sketch, this speed-painting was all the more impressive. He was decisive and relentless, swapping brushes and mixing colors as if by sleight of hand, as if he'd painted this cat a hundred times. It was over in less than an hour. None of us had budged.

His cat wore a coat of a dozen colors, as if catching the dawns and dusks of a dozen days. It was stitched of tiny downstrokes, strokes placed so quickly as to preclude their being anything but random, but with a final effect so perfect as to make the notion absurd. The slightest shifts in the frequency of certain tones gave depth and shading and definition that completely belied the childish outline he retained from the sketch. The feline eyes were nearly human, blue and condescending, piercing and alive. Greens and purples lifted from the colors of its coat and swirled like a conjurer's smoke to fill the page. And such was the effect on the boys, as the conjurer lured them to their easels.

He must have produced that template for them fifty or sixty times over the next several days, always on the black paper, and always with a single pigment stick. Every cat sat tall and looked straight on, each with its tail to the side and curled slightly upwards, waiting for the boys and their pigment sticks. The artist, his pipe puffing like Mary Anne the steamshovel, worked with the Parenteau boys on their palettes, just as he'd worked with Blake. In no time the cats took their colorations from the many things we saw around us, each specimen shaped identically but colored like no other. He omitted the whiskers and eyes from his sketches, leaving those to be shaped entirely by the boys. Each cat took on a distinct persona on that basis as well, with whiskers thick and thin, long and short, droopy and upturned; and eyes sleepy or confronting, focused or wandering, slitted or blotted.

I rather liked my earlier easel design, and, looking to contribute, I began a production run of new easels in graduated heights for Blake and each of the Parenteau boys. By noon the next day I'd completed all four. We spread them like sentries on the deck, and the boys fell into a pattern of "painting" for an hour or so every day after lunch, the artist flitting around attentively in the background.

And so, in a hail of hilarity – the Parenteau boys making a secondary art in the coining of fraternal insults – we acquired a very substantial collection of wildly pigmented cats, in textured patterns from all the spectrum, the black underlay adding depth in every work. I knew what a sacrifice it was for the artist, giving up that hour of precious sunlight from his own work most days – he'd just begun a study of the apple trees next door. But to look at him, it didn't seem a sacrifice at all. And he didn't seem so much a teacher, or even a mentor, as he did a collaborator or an artist's agent, encouraging production and emerging elements in each boy's personal style, as he generally phrased it. I couldn't help but think how different this artist was from the madman I'd seen in the truck. Blake progressed from calico curls to big spots. They gave the impression of moons orbiting his unwitting cats. Kevin was the master of the addled cat, cats with X's for eyes and tongues lolling out. All kinds of stellar bodies lurked in his backgrounds – big round suns with rays like spider arms, giant asymmetrical stars, and multiple moons in purples and reds. Jamie was a master of painstaking, intricate scotch plaids. One of his cats smoked a pipe, and didn't look the least bit out of place doing so. And Koby, who'd spent the most time studying the artist's particular techniques, picked up on one element of his style: behind his cats, the backdrops swirled of colors lifted from the palettes of their fantastical multi-hued coats.

On the third of those afternoon deck sessions the roar of what we thought was a chopper blew down our road. Both shock and awe were in play – we were deafened, certainly, and the contrast to the normal forest quiet heightened the effect for us. We all turned to watch it go by – it was a car, a hot rod – and, rather than going by, it turned right into our driveway. I'm not a car junkie but this one was unmistakable – a late-sixties Pontiac GTO. I hollered that out to the boys, though no one could possibly have heard. While noise was the car's signature feature, it had the makings of a visual swagger as well. The GTO design was showy in itself, and in this case air shocks lifted the body high over gleaming five-slot mag wheels. But its coat was sickly brown and spotted with priming patches, suggesting a paint job yet to come. Tinted windows precluded my seeing the driver. He pulled decisively into a spot against the stone wall. Only after several more agonizing seconds did the car sputter into silence. The cat bounded from behind the stone wall, across the driveway and onto the porch, crouching behind the rail.

The car stood silent for a moment, and then three of its doors opened in unison. The way the driver had pulled into that spot, I figured he must have had some familiarity with the place, and sure enough, out came a tall, lean character I identified as Bobby Bethune. I hadn't run across him since the march. He approached with an affected nonchalance that allowed the other two to come around the car and fall into formation behind him. They seemed to shuffle rather than walk across the gravel, making crunching sounds and raising a short puff of dust. I remember thinking it almost laughable. Bobby made a show of ogling the house, as if conducting an official inspection. He led his companions up the stairs and out onto the deck with an assurance as if he still lived there. He'd put on some muscle since I'd seen him last.

"Hello, Bobby," I said. "Nice car."

He looked past me and answered, "When did you turn this place into a fairy drawing school?"

That shocked me pretty well into silence. There was a time when I would have knocked him down, right there on the spot. But since I'd been a single parent I'd started considering things a little more. I'd become a little less instinctive. I hadn't remembered it until now, but I recognized his ugly sneer from the last time I'd seen him, from the march, when he'd kissed me on both cheeks. It struck me for the first time that his appearance there had been a charade, some twisted Judas act I'd been too dazed to comprehend. Now his crazy eyes were fixed on the easels. He'd begun a sarcastic walk-through – "Oh, there's a pretty cat! There's a nice little pussy! That one's the cat's meow!" – while his buddies, with not a brain between them, stood smirking at the rail.

With the kids on the deck, I was inclined not to accelerate things if I didn't have to, and I continued to play the backwoods Hamlet. Blake was not much affected, but I noticed that the Parenteau boys were cowed – Koby in particular. Either he'd always been afraid of Bobby, or he was getting old enough now to feel threatened for the first time. The artist, who'd taken an immediate and tangible disliking to the visitors, was the first of us to speak.

"Perhaps the gentlemen would care to move along."

"No, the gentlemen would not care to move along," Bobby said in a poor parody of a European accent. "Freak."

Something took hold of me then, and I steered Bobby to one side with a grab of his shirt. In a low voice meant only for him, I said, "You need to leave. Get off my porch, and take your dumbass friends with you."

It hardly seemed to register. He didn't answer or make a move one way or the other. He still hadn't even looked at me. Once I'd started I'd gotten pretty fired up – the blood was actually pulsing in my ears. But I guessed that he needed to dawdle a bit to regain some standing with his buddies. I managed my agitation just enough to give them those few seconds, to let them gather themselves up in the nearly natural flow of things. They stepped off the porch and headed down the walk, with the same affected nonchalance they'd shown on their approach. Bobby lingered for a moment at my truck, eyeing its rear windshield while his buddies circled to the far side of the GTO. As he opened his own car door, he turned and looked straight at me.

"Looks like you need to update your stick figures," he said.

Or at least that's what I think he said. And then the car roared to life, and they were gone.

Chapter 20

APPLE TREES ON A SUMMER AFTERNOON

When the noise of the GTO had died off, Kevin bent over, picked something imaginary off the deck and said, "Oh, good! I was hoping I'd find my eardrum again!" That got a few chuckles. None of them came from me, but looking back on it now, it was a pretty good line. He was just the right kid for that moment. I, on the other hand, was just the wrong adult. I remember thinking I needed to say something, to frame for them what had just happened. But first I needed to frame it for myself. I couldn't muster a sentence until I did, and as it turned out, that would be a while in coming. As I floundered there in silence I could feel the artist's stare boring in, like when he'd first walked up our road. And then he broke it off and said the strangest thing.

"Though I am often in the depths of misery," – he paused here – "there is still calmness, pure harmony, and music inside me." As if to dispel any notion that he might explain the remark, he picked up his jug and took a long swallow.

For the second time in as many minutes, I wasn't quite sure what I'd heard. Was he quoting Psalms or something? I hadn't taken him for a religious man. The boys looked equally perplexed, but before things could get any more awkward, and before Kevin could think of some clever retort – he was, after all, a young boy and not yet a fully developed wit – the artist snatched up a handful of pastel sticks and approached the nearest easel. In prior classes he'd never drawn directly onto the boys' work. And beyond the templates, he'd never worked with the pastel sticks. But now he did both, as if they were perfectly natural for him. We watched him work, too shell-shocked for our normal trepidation on the point. As when he'd painted his *Cat*, he made no objection.

This though was a much different spectacle than *Cat*. That had been pure showmanship. This was inspiration with a different bent, showmanship once removed. He worked through some uncanny artistic ventriloquy, effecting the voice that had come before him. However rudimentary the scribblings – and that first easel was Blake's – he blended his own marks as if possessed by the child himself. His contributions were instant and impactful, but coded to and completely embedded in the childish idiom of the existing work. A few scribbles served somehow to harmonize the colors, the light, the shadowing. After a minute or so he shifted to the next easel. There too, he dove like a master polyglot into the language at hand, adopting Kevin's particular and juvenile motif. Subtle shadings rounded the edges and raised the animal from the flat of the paper. Later, when we reviewed all four collaborative cats, we couldn't identify a single of his strokes – he'd left no discernible tracks. His additions didn't change the artistic approach or the apparent skill level of any of the drawings. It somehow just made them work. The boys were amazed by the subtle transformation of their cats – as if they themselves had stepped to another tier in their development. The artist loaded a fresh sheet of the black paper onto each easel. The boys started again, each picking a particular palette. And each did the best work he'd done to date.

The artist lingered longer than usual on the deck that day. It was another hour before he concluded the lesson with his usual bow to the students. In spite of the Bethune scare, it had been the best session they'd spent together. Kevin and Blake returned spirited bows. Koby smiled ironically. Jamie colored and turned away. It was, in short, a return to normalcy, all in keeping with the most recent routines. The artist walked back to his post before the apple trees. The boys drifted home, one by one, staggering their departures as they always did. And I lay down to settle Blake for his afternoon nap, though my mind was as far from settled as it had been in a long time.

If that was the game, I would have to play it. It was outrageous enough to come up on my deck like that and bully a bunch of children, but that last comment was beyond imagining. *"Looks like you need to update your stick figures."* Had I heard it wrong, or could he really have said that? And if so, why? For that matter, why any of it? That level of hostility – both on the deck and in the comment – seemed completely out of left field. He probably didn't like city people. And he probably blamed us for the loss of the cabin, though he himself had caused it with the break-in and restitution order. Still, the hostility he'd brought today went well beyond not liking us, and well beyond what I would consider a reasonable degree of displaced anger. And the march – what had really happened there? When he'd shown up in the line I'd taken it at face value. Given the circumstances, it had been impossible not to. Now I really did take it as a prank. Was there an audience he'd played for, friends who'd queued with him in the line that night? I wasn't even close to remembering that, one way or the other. Was he just unstable and angry and ignorant, someone who needed hard boundaries, and nothing more? Or was this all something more sinister? I may have been overreaching, but his strange performance that afternoon seemed to point at something far darker.

I could hardly blame Blake for taking a while to go to sleep. The vibe on my side of the bed was anything but peaceful. It took all my concentration just to lie still. But at last he dropped off. And the second he did I went straight for the logbook. It seemed crazy I hadn't seen that car before. It was something I couldn't possibly have overlooked, but I'd never seen or heard it before that day. Not on the road, and not parked at the Bethune house, though I'd been by there on half a dozen walks. I'd been so shocked by Bobby's parting comment that I'd come away with just the first three numbers of the plate. But they were enough to confirm that I had no record of his GTO, by plate number or by description. Either he'd just bought it, or had it out on the road, or shut up in the garage, every time I'd been by. I turned it all over again, the house sale, the march, the scene on the porch, the parting comment. Something strange was in play, and I was churning with the worst case scenario. But I had nothing really to go on that way – it was only speculation, and an angry, irrational speculation at that. But even if only at face value, today's scene, the comment in particular, required a response.

I thought then of the car-bashing fundraisers I'd seen as a kid: the donated old clunker car, the sledgehammer, first swings to the highest bidders, five bucks a swing thereafter; the crowd uneasy at first, cheering the first tentative blows, working themselves into it and finally going crazy when one angry man – it always takes one angry man – goes into a froth with a dozen savage hacks and the car begins to pass beyond the familiar. In the end, a couple hundred bucks for Pop Warner football, the crowd slipping away, and the unloved, bludgeoned heap hauled off to the scrapyard. Such an evenhanded bash might suffice here. It would set an ample boundary, quasi-anonymous but acutely personal.

"We will finish the scribing tonight?"

I jumped nearly out of my skin. It was the artist, not ten feet away, speaking through the screen door. I had no idea how he'd gotten there – I'd just seen him in the Parenteaus' field, painting with his back to me. It was my turn for the delayed response.

"Yes, that would be great. Thanks."

He headed back off the porch, and I watched him down the path, through the cut in the stone wall, and back to his easel. It was no surprise that he wanted to do the work – he'd mentioned it a couple times already. He seemed to feel indebted about his room and board, though the way I saw it you could hardly consider a tent in the yard a room, and the single painting he'd given us already was worth a year of meals – assuming he didn't pry it off and paint on the back, which wasn't going to happen on my watch. But the timing of the suggestion seemed remarkable on a couple fronts. I'd never seen him voluntarily interrupt a work session, except for the noon lessons. But that is exactly what he'd done, and after an especially long noon lesson. And in doing it just then he'd thrown me a line in the heart of my darkest place, where my most generous thoughts revolved around a sledgehammer and an antique GTO. In his odd way, he was trying to hold me together. From a simple logistical standpoint, which he well understood, once I'd committed to the evening scribing I needed to build the scaffolding. And with Blake in sleep, it had to be now.

What followed, oddly enough, was one of the longest, sleepiest stretches of the summer. I swirled in the Bethune vortex, but everything around us seemed to thicken and stick, as if some strange soupy atmosphere had settled down over the pines. The scaffolding came together almost subconsciously – time had stuttered and slowed to the point that I finished in much the same early afternoon light I'd noticed when I'd begun. Blake napped extra long, woke up foggy and sluggish, and stayed that way for hours. And the artist seemed to labor for an eternity, as if the sun had stood still, granting him back the time he'd lost to the lessons. I'd catch the occasional glimpse of him through the west windows, fully engrossed, tilted slightly at the waist, the tip of his brush wagging like the plume of a feather pen. I saw him take a pull from his jug, but the brush wagged on, even as water dripped from his chin. Not once did he slacken.

And so it was that, for all the interruptions of the day, *Apple Trees on a Summer Afternoon* came in before dark. It was the second of the apple tree series. I was so blown away this time that I stopped thinking about Bobby Bethune for a minute or two. His pines had been course and textured, but also, by their nature, straight as mast poles. His trees at the beaver pond had been slightly more aberrant – harried by the water and by fifty-pound gnawing rodentia on one side, and by encroaching forest giants on the other, they seemed to skulk and slink of their own accord. But the apple trees, as he'd seen them, were deviant and misshapen from their lowest beginnings, from their dubious bases through their lithesome trunks and knuckled arms and bony fingers. They undulated in a lewd and horrible tribal rhythm; forking unnaturally at every turn, as if bent and broken and mistreated from the first sprig. They bore leafy bouquets in their writhing limbs, enticing and deadly, proffered like bunches of poisoned candy. At their feet flowed a meadow of flame, a multi-toned molten river breaching its banks to overrun this devil's orchard.

Our gallery had become Smaug's lair, a den of unthinkable riches, an embarrassment of outrageous excess. Any two of those paintings would overwhelm a good-sized room, and any one of them would stupefy a smaller space. But we'd packed two on the mantel – *Pine Trees on a Summer Morning* and *Pine Trees Before the Dusk*; two on the wall – *Pondscape at Dawn* and *Beaver on Napkin* (I'd taken the liberty of naming the pilfered sketch); and five more freestanding, all in our little living room. *Garden at Noon with Figure, Pondscape in the Afternoon, Cat, Meadow with Apple Trees,* and *Apple Trees on a Summer Afternoon* – they circled on their crude hand-cut easels, angling in on themselves like patrons at an overcrowded cocktail party, contorting politely to clear the couch, the chair, the bed, the end tables, the woodstove. Blake and I had to work our way through the little grove of easels just to get to his bed. He liked it that way – the scene had a *Where the Wild Things Are* kind of flair. But here was one more reason to get him moved upstairs. We desperately needed the space. Much as I wanted to slip out and bludgeon that GTO, it was a far better idea to let things settle for a day or two. Quasi-anonymity required it. I'd be better off finishing the house project while I still had the artist's help. For all my concerns about exploiting his labor, I couldn't move on without him.

Chapter 21

UP ON THE PLANKS

The makeshift scaffolding – a gangway of planks on hand-made saw-horses – made for tight quarters. As the artist and I bent under the sloped ceiling, it seemed I'd spend the whole night walking sideways. Putting Blake to bed after his long afternoon nap had required several side-angled excursions through the easels – to the kitchen and back, to the bathroom and back, to the bookshelf and back. And now I was scuttling once again, past the artist and back again in our rotations on the planks. He'd wedge by me to the wall to make his sketches, and I'd lurch back with the screwgun, a shuffle we'd repeat dozens of times during the work.

That scuttling sensation went beyond the physical maneuvers. I felt generally constricted that night as I brushed past the quasi-boarder I knew only as Willem or WG. He'd been with us for a week and a half, endearing himself to my boy and to the Parenteau boys, and he was still a complete mystery. I'd questioned him directly, at least at the beginning. I'd told him a good chunk of my story, hoping he'd come back with something, anything. But at the end of the day I knew only what I'd observed, what I'd seen directly. Part of that observation was the gift of what I, for one, considered a brilliant piece of art, uniquely customized to our home. It was just one of the many we'd been lucky enough to

117

have him paint on the premises. And here was such an artist, tutoring kids and donating his highly skilled labor, late at night, to a project as mundane as hanging our sheetrock. The unspoken condition of his largesse, made clear enough from the beginning, was my respect for his anonymity. It would seem a breach for me to badger him now, after so many days of unspoken compliance. He was not going to volunteer anything – that seemed clear. We'd shared strings of meals, campfires and chores without his ever crossing, or even approaching, that line. Either I accepted him on the face of what little I knew, or I didn't. Either I accepted that he was not an ongoing risk, or I didn't. And in an unspoken way, I'd already staked a position, for myself and for Blake.

The Parenteaus, however, were another story. Karl and Betty were painfully overdue for an introduction. I'd discussed the artist with them early in his stay, but he'd been around for all that time since, camping, traipsing through the woods, bathing in the lake. And though he was pretty discrete with all that, he was still hard to miss, perched for entire days on our deck, on the side of the road, and, most recently, right out in their field. With their boys now in his tutelage, the introduction was particularly pressing. We were already to the point where their parents could, quite rightfully, have charged me with a reckless abuse of their trust.

Clearly, I'd had my reasons for holding off. Eccentricity is not necessarily a bad thing – though our strange trip to the art store had knocked me back some. And the artist could be quite charming, even gentle in stretches. But at other times he'd be unresponsive, dismissive, and abrasive. It could irritate the hell out of you. His accent was foreign to us, but that was the least of his communication problems. When he chose to answer at all, he took so long it couldn't help but be a little offputting. And it didn't come off as a language problem, but as a focus problem. He just had a different way of processing things. Grooming and dress were further problems. I believe he washed his

118

clothes in the lake on occasion, but the effect was never quite optimal. And, of course, there was the elephant in the room, the voids that were unacceptable in most any social context, the void that was his last name, the void that was his history, the void that was his intent. But for all of that, it was getting awkward enough in our little neighborhood that if the meeting didn't happen soon, and go reasonably well, things could come to a head.

"Willem, do you still have any interest in painting from the lake? I mean, if we could borrow the pontoon, would you like to look across the water to the shoreline?"

We'd been half an hour without exchanging more than a few sentences, so in this case his delayed response seemed perfectly normal.

"Yes, I would very much like a day on the water."

"So maybe you should meet the Parenteaus, and we can set that up – especially since you've been nice enough to work with their kids. What do you say I invite them down on Saturday morning? We can put on an exhibit of the kids' work, and maybe they can take a look at yours too."

He was not thrilled to have the Parenteaus review his work, but agreed not to resist it in the context of their children's exhibit. We discussed the logistics of the event, and when we'd reached something like an agreement we drifted back into our own thoughts. Mine had become too familiar.

Bobby Bethune deserved a beating. He was way over the line, and it was simple justice. But I was in no position to go around battering people. I was a single parent, and, theoretically at least, a teacher in good standing at the high school. I didn't need an assault charge. By the same logic I couldn't go around bashing people's cars either. But if I did it right I could send the message without getting pinned for it. It was simply logistics. There was no hint of a moral dilemma, except for the great big obvious one: if I was really dealing with the worst case, then the car was only an afterthought. But I could never prove that hunch, to myself, or to anyone else. Not even close. One thing I could confirm, in any case, was what had actually been said. My best adult witness, though not a native speaker, was conveniently at hand.

"When Bobby got back in his car today – did you happen to hear him say we ought to update our stick figures?"

Silence.

"I was deaf a little from the car." Pause. "But, yes, perhaps I did hear that. Stick figures are the small characters on the rear glass of the truck?"

"Yes."

"I thought that."

"And he was looking right at them when he said it. I assume by 'update' he meant that I should peel my wife off the window on account of her being dead. I didn't want to ask the boys, but I'm curious as to whether you thought the same thing."

"I thought that maybe, yes."

Not exactly iron-clad confirmation, but it was something. Neither of us said anything as we worked through another two pieces.

"You knew him from before," he said.

"His family owned the house before we did. He got in some trouble and ran up a big chunk of debt, which, I found out later, is why they had to sell it. He grew up here and probably liked the place as much as we do. He didn't seem to like the prospect of our taking it at the time. And he probably likes it even less now, with their having moved to such a depressing place and with everything cleaned up a lot nicer here."

"Perhaps then he speaks unkindly simply for that."

"A little over the top, I think. But that would make more sense than coming over here and acting up if he was actually the guy who hit her. Especially with a muscle car like that – and one that's so obviously had body work. But for some reason I think that's exactly what happened. He's had a year to get that car painted, but he doesn't even bother. He flaunts it. I think he's the one who ran her down. And he doesn't mind me knowing it."

"And you would like knowing that."

I had to think about that for a moment. "Yeah, I guess I would."

Chapter 22

THE GOLDEN SPIKE

Those scribing sessions always left us coated in sheetrock dust. It was the kind of dust you couldn't just brush off — white and powdery, very fine, but obvious on dark clothing. I don't know why it hadn't occurred to me before, but the end of that night's session struck me as an opportunity to offer my laundry facilities, and to do so without being offensive. The artist, as it happened, had no interest in operating the machines himself. But he seemed happy enough with the concept of a dropoff service. And so, by arrangement, a small bundle appeared at the door just after dark the next day — his daily wear, one change of underwear and socks, and his jacket, bundled and tied in a cloth. With only a slight hit to my self-esteem, I washed and dried his clothes. I started to fold them, then, on an impulse, washed and dried them again. I left them back outside, where he picked them up just after dawn.

And so, on the morning of the Parenteaus' visit, he was more preened than I'd ever seen him. He had a fresher scent about him, and his clothes had lost a bit of their drifter's sheen. His shoes looked oiled. He'd buttoned his jacket tightly at the neck, despite the coming heat. As we'd agreed, we set the boys' art under the porch roof, clamping rows of pigmented cats between pairs of ten-foot strapping sections. This made four ten-foot displays, like strings of banners, one string for each boy. These we mounted on a makeshift stand, the artist working right with me and proving himself again quite adept with his ball peen hammer. He perspired alarmingly, but ignored my suggestion to remove the jacket.

The Parenteau boys arrived soon after lunch. Each was happy to admire his own work and criticize that of his brothers. Just as the artist shooed them to their easels, their parents came walking down the driveway. I stood to meet them on the porch, just as I'd done the first day with the artist. Betty's reaction wasn't much different than his had been – she walked right by me to the deck. Karl gave me an apologetic shrug and followed her to the easels. The boys, in turn, could hardly be bothered to acknowledge their parents, though I made Blake stop his work and shake their hands. I then introduced the artist. He bowed formally. Karl chuckled, not rudely or with any condescension, but simply in keeping with his good nature. He made a half bow back.

"The boys are excited with all the artwork," Betty said, directly to the artist. As expected, he didn't immediately respond. I'd been dreading this first exchange, but not nearly enough, I realized. I'd mentioned to the Parenteaus that he could be halting in his speech, but I saw now how painfully inadequate that warning had been. I waited to see how Betty would handle the empty space between question and reply, if a reply were forthcoming at all. He stared straight ahead, perspiring and unspeaking. She knitted her brows, looked away, looked back.

"Each boy has a good eye for light, and for color," he said at last. "It is my great pleasure to overlook them."

It was an unfortunate remark, even if well intentioned. Betty sighed, and we circled back to the exhibit. I was relieved that at least he'd spoken.

"Lots of cats," she said, in a voice that betrayed some bewilderment.

The artist's pause was shorter this time. "Yes, it is good to have repetition on the same sketch in order to experiment with color. They are all improving with each day." Now he's got it going, I thought.

And then, completely unsolicited, he spoke again: "The older boys are just begun to understand shadow and light." Old Willem was starting to really sling it.

"Not from what I can tell," said Kevin, who was not technically one of the older boys. "They still seem pretty stupid to me."

"Kevin!" Betty gasped.

A string of insults followed among the three, over the objections of both parents. The artist continued, completely unflustered by the five competing voices, each of them louder than his.

"We will move on shortly, to sketching and to still-lifes."

After another minute of family banter, there began a more formal tour of the work, with discussion of each boy's particular strengths and signature features.

"Wow, Kevin. I really like this one," said Betty, pointing immediately to the one the artist had doctored.

"There's a surprise," said Koby, rolling his eyes at the others. "And which one of mine do you think is the best?"

"Oh, definitely this one here," she said, pointing again to a doctored work.

The boys all howled with laughter, but she carried on, completely unphased.

"What brings you to Pinewoods, Willem?"

Uh-oh, I thought. Here comes the background check.

Pause.

"The light here is very good."

She scowled. "I understand you walked in. Do you always travel on foot?"

"Actually we drove to the art store just the other day," I said.

Betty gave me a quick look and returned to the artist.

"And where do you live? How long are you planning to stay?"

Pause.

I was terrified that the artist would completely stonewall her at this point. But at the same time I had a morbid curiosity as to whether she could extract any more information in this one interview than I'd managed in a week and a half.

Silence. Double silence. He was not going to answer. Betty glared at me — it was clear I'd put her children in the hands of a degenerate and felon.

"Look at the coloration in that cat," I said, idiotically, pointing at random to one of Blake's pieces. Jamie jumped in to the rescue.

"Yeah, Mom, look at the palette Blake used in this one. They're the colors of Mister Willem's hair."

The artist removed his hat — his hair was slicked back, quite possibly with the same material he'd used on his shoes, one of his painting products perhaps — and posed by the cat with a stern and feline expression. Everyone laughed. Betty was the last to let herself go, but in the end she laughed as much as anyone. The crisis seemed to have passed.

I invited them in to the Gallery. Karl stood at the first easel, *Pondscape in the Afternoon*. "Whoa," he said quietly, and then his voice trailed off. His moustache twitched. His feet shuffled. Beyond that, he didn't move at all.

Betty, on the other hand, zipped through the collection. "Wow, that's a lot of color," she said. "That's our apple orchard. I've seen you out there a few times. I should get you to paint our house. Do you paint dogs? There's a lot of money in dogs. You could do a practice painting of our dog, show it around, and get some customers that way. There's a man at the markets — I see him at the fairgrounds too — he sketches dogs for people, right on the spot. Or he takes appointments to paint them later. He likes to paint from pictures. You give him a picture of your dog, a picture you like that really shows their personality, and in a week or two you have your painting. They're good enough to frame and put right up in your living room. And he's not cheap. One painting is a couple hundred dollars. More than some people even pay for their dogs. I'm sure you'd be as good as he is."

"I don't paint dogs," said the artist. A quick enough response that time.

"Well, you paint cats. I'm assuming this one is yours," she said, gesturing to the only *Cat* in the Gallery. He neither confirmed nor denied it. "I can see right here that you've painted at least one cat. They would have to be more realistic – if they're paying for it, they'll want it realistic. But if you can paint a cat I would think you could paint a dog. Granted, some people have cats – to each his own. But for an artist the real money's in dogs."

Silence.

"When do you want the pontoon?" Karl asked.

That question came as a great relief, and it was about the last thing I remember from the exhibit that day. I remember being happy that we'd survived the introduction, and happy that we'd secured the pontoon. None of the Parenteaus had mentioned the Bethune incident – I couldn't tell if the boys had told their parents or not. I'd flirted with the idea of asking Betty if she knew anything more about Bobby, but decided against it so as to raise as little suspicion as possible once I'd reconfigured the GTO. I figure Blake must have gone home with the Parenteaus, because I remember taking a drive by the Bethune place to just that end.

One car sat outside the garage. I'd seen it there before and guessed that it belonged to the parents. Commandeering the only garage port would be pretty impudent of the stay-at-home son, but not inconsistent with what little I knew of him. There wouldn't be a lot of space in there, not around a full-bodied vehicle like a GTO. But the pitched roof line had the potential to offset that. If there weren't any joists in the way I'd have the best clearance, and the best leverage, standing right on the car – on the hood, on the roof, and on the trunk. From those three stations I could slam the hammer straight down, just like splitting wood. I needed to see how that garage was framed, and, of course, I needed to confirm that it actually housed the GTO. There was a side door with three-over-three windows, but I couldn't exactly get out and look things over in broad daylight. It was dangerous enough driving by as slowly as I had. I'd get another look later.

The artist and I finished the sheetrocking that night. It was the most physical of the labor I'd asked of him. We were on the higher wall sections, and he had to hold the sheets overhead while I screwed them in place. Sheetrock is heavy and awkward in any case. Throw in flimsy scaffolding and a cathedral ceiling, with the walls tilting in, and you have a pretty miserable job. I felt terrible using him this way, but our progress was so tangible it seemed to buoy us both. "Thirty-two square feet per sheet," I said, and unlike most of my inanities, which he'd persistently ignored, this one earned a nod in response.

We set the last sheet just before midnight. I held up the final screw before driving it in. "The golden spike," I said. I'm sure he had no idea what I was talking about, but rather than taking the time to explain, I just shook his hand, thanked him, and encouraged him to turn in. It was late, and we were due for our pontoon run first thing in the morning. I really was very grateful for his help, but my mind was already down the road.

I figured I had twenty seconds from the first bang of the sledgehammer until I had to be out. It would take me ten shots just for the glass – windshields, windows, headlights, taillights – and I needed the nose cone, the grill, and at least one shot into every panel on the car. If I couldn't get into the garage without waking people up, I wouldn't have time to finish the job. Breaking in would probably be too loud – I needed to know if they kept the side door locked at night. I'd never noticed a dog at the Bethune place, but I needed to confirm that too. It all required a better look.

The artist was still there, sitting on the scaffolding, his legs dangling like a child's, watching what I'd do next. I knew it'd be a while before I felt like sleeping. And, distracted as I was, having Blake's room so nearly finished was a big consideration. I decided to press on. I grabbed the mesh tape and set some strips of it over a few of the joints. The artist seemed curious, as if he'd never done any taping or spackling. Before I started spreading the joint compound I showed him the makeshift palette I used to hold it. I didn't do that to recruit his help, but because I thought it a piece of common ground between us. The job required a palette, just like his did. He didn't seem particularly enthralled, but he didn't get up and leave either. I opened the five-gallon bucket and glopped some joint compound onto the palette. I scooped some with the spackle knife and smeared it over the mesh, into the joints, and over the screwheads, smoothing as best I could. He seemed more interested now, and before I could scoop the next batch he gestured for the palette and the knife. He tucked the palette into his left elbow, took the knife, and repeated what I'd just done, a little better, actually, than I had. And just like that, we were back to working in tandem. I'd lay the tape, and he'd cover it with a smooth spread of joint compound, doing professional grade work from the first go. I was happy to have his help, and I hoped he might benefit as well. I imagined some satisfaction from teamwork, and from executing a job he could naturally do well. How ridiculous that seems now, as if he didn't already have a job he could do well!

Regardless of what either of us were actually thinking, we pressed on, and we finished the room. Once again I shook his hand. This time he gave me a bow and headed out to his tent. It was just past two in the morning – just about the time I'd set out on the night I'd beat the GTO.

I stifled the impulse to do it right then – the extra scouting had to be done, and I needed a few more days gone by to strengthen my "plausible deniability". But now was the perfect time for the night scout, and, I realized, for a full run-through. Nearly intoxicated with this sudden decisiveness, I changed into my dark mission gear, chugged some water, and ran downstairs for the sledgehammer. I took a moment to confirm that Blake was sound asleep, and held my breath as I set the screen door behind me. It crossed my mind with pleasant effect that this would be his last night sleeping in the Gallery. I set my watch to time the trip, slipped quietly by the artist's tent, and was running when I hit the pavement, cradling the head of the hammer like a football. Fifteen minutes later I was slowing my breath against the side of the Bethune's garage.

What I found there was all good. No barking, check. Side door unlocked, check. GTO nestled inside, check. Framing open to the ceiling, check. With the right moon I'd have just enough light.

Chapter 23

AN UNEXPECTED SWIM

I felt like hell when Blake came in the next morning, but somehow the artist had gotten himself up before dawn. By the time Blake and I brought breakfast onto the deck, his tent was folded, as always, near the door, and he'd completed his morning walk. He approached us with his jacket flung jauntily over one shoulder, more suited to film an Old Spice commercial than to launch a moldy old party pontoon. Not only was he wide awake, he was as upbeat as I'd seen him, bowing and darting about, holding doors, carrying plates, folding and setting the napkins. Blake, the only one of us who'd gotten a decent night's sleep, was somehow the one to have woken up on the grouchy side. Puffy eyes and extreme bedhead – a full-on pompadour in this case – generally indicated that he needed some space. But the artist seemed less than perceptive on the point. He peppered the child with morning greetings, and comments about beautiful light, and inquiries about his sleep. I deflected as much as I could while trying to orchestrate the breakfast, but it was all I could do to keep Blake from sticking a fork in his leg.

I could see that the artist had streamlined his equipment for the outing. The quiver had been pared to the most pressing supplies, and his rucksack was much lightened – I imagined it held his paint supplies and water jug only. I handed him a sandwich. He bowed and placed it in the depths of the sack. Blake and I were in our swim trunks. Our thought was to put him in position, anchor the pontoon, swim back, and return for him at the end of his workday.

Karl had left the key in the ignition, just as he'd promised. I hoisted Blake over and jumped across myself. I pull-started the engine without any trouble. The artist untied us from the mooring and bent low to push us off. I expected him to hop over as soon as we were off the dock, but he kept pushing. "Jump on," I said. He looked at me, and seemed to hear, but he kept his hands low on the pontoon rail, pushing as before, and before I could say anything more he was leaning too far out, beginning to triangulate out over the water. The angle at his waist continued to broaden as his body weight drove the pontoon steadily from the dock. I hopped over to help, but the situation was unrecoverable. He was splayed nearly horizontal, in a plank position, as if poised for pushups over the water.

"Give me the quiver," I said. He managed to lift that arm, and I pulled the quiver free just as he collapsed. His straw hat bobbed on the surface – that was all that was left of him. I grabbed it, and he sputtered back up. He threw an arm over the pontoon deck, and I grabbed at the rucksack. I directed him to the ladder, and in a few seconds he was standing next to us, streaming water like a statue in a fountain.

"I'll get you a towel," I said. We'd left the towels on the dock, where I'd assumed they'd be needed. I reversed the pontoon and made a quick jump over and back to grab one. The artist removed his shoes and stripped to the waist as we puttered out into the lake. He was broad-shouldered, but thinner than I'd thought, all ribs and chicken wings.

"You did well to save the canvas," he said, eyes already trained on the shoreline. He made no further reference to having fallen in the lake. I'm not sure it had really even registered with him. Blake was too polite to comment, and, mostly on his account, I didn't say anything either. The artist toweled off absent-mindedly, directing us steadily to the vantage point he'd picked from the moment he'd climbed back aboard. "Go, go. More. A tiny more. Halt the craft."

I reversed, threw the anchor, and killed the engine. The artist was already kneeling to his bundles. He laid his brushes and his easel in the sun, and began his familiar elfin flurry – Blake and I liked watching this part – assembling the easel and the stretcher and tacking the canvas. I surveyed the shore, trying to guess what exactly he had in mind. He pulled out his pencil to sketch. Within a few strokes I could see it was where the feeder creek entered the lake, downstream from the Dominion. The junction had been engineered long ago, with great stones piled in a wall on the east side. Blake and I lingered as long as we dared. At the artist's first glance our way I asked: "Is the sandwich dry?" When he nodded yes, I wished him luck and dove off the boat. Blake followed suit, and in a few minutes we were on the dock.

Blake and I spent the rest of the morning building a few more easels. We always tried to stay a couple easels ahead of our artist in residence, though I was running low on scrap wood, and my output, as a result, was getting progressively shoddier. During Blake's nap, I picked up where we'd left off taping and spackling upstairs. I was determined to finish Blake's room, and when his nap ran late I was able to do that. Much later, when the sun was nearing the western tree line, we walked back to check on the artist. I hollered over from the dock. He gave us a quick glance, then turned right back to the canvas. I took that to mean he wasn't ready, but we stood and stared for a minute longer, until he glanced at us again and, without a word, turned again to his canvas. He might at least have given Blake a wave, I thought, but Blake didn't seem bothered in the least. We walked back home.

An hour later we walked down for another check. Then we had dinner and checked again. By that time, Blake, well-napped as he was, had had enough of traipsing through the woods – he rode back on my shoulders. I revived him with a dessert of graham crackers and milk, and we headed down for the fourth time, this time in fading light. The entire yard was deep in shadow. Passage through the woods was slower this time, dark and difficult. Sometimes kids just don't want to be picked up, even though they can barely put one foot in front of another. This was one of those times. He walked on his own, drunk with fatigue. I took the lead, holding low-hanging branches clear for him. At last we popped into the clear. We didn't see the artist at first, but he was out there, supine on the pontoon deck. The sky was layered in neon pink-and-orange strips, clouds ruffled like a roll of thick-wale corduroy and rolled out as far as we could see. I knew we were short on time, but the colors seemed to lift Blake's spirits. So I sat on the dock watching the sky with him for five or ten minutes. Then I swam out to the pontoon, turning around every five or six strokes to make sure Blake was still as I'd left him. The artist had packed up his things, but he hardly moved when I climbed aboard. I asked him how his day had gone, and he didn't say a word. The rude bastard, I thought. It was too dark to get much of a look at the canvas. The rest of the color ran out of the sky as I puttered us in.

We would have to haul the canvas through the forest in almost total darkness. I'd brought a flashlight, but this was shaping up to be more of a project than I could handle. The artist was having an episode – for some reason he still refused to speak. He leaned the canvas against a tree, and when I went to pick it up, he stopped me and set it back without explanation. Was he always like this on short sleep? We went through this sequence twice. He seemed to want to leave the painting out for the night, presumably thinking it unsafe to haul it through the woods. Blake, meanwhile, was completely shot, and starting to lose the plot – there was no way he was walking back on his own. So I left the artist on the shore and the canvas against the tree, and hauled Blake on my shoulders to the Parenteaus' for help. He pressed his head tight to mine as we ducked through clusters of low-hanging pine. In a few minutes we had Karl and the three boys, with three flashlights, hoofing it back down the path.

I could barely make it out, but the painting was still leaning, like a churchyard tombstone, at the base of the tree. As we came around, the boys trained their lights to look, and, after a quick glance for the artist, who was nowhere to be seen, I added my light to the mix. The beams were disorienting at first, crossing and doubling back like little searchlights. But then they settled, and the painting came into focus. We all stood for a moment to take it in.

The stone wall he'd pictured was the remnant of a battered fortress, left to molder and slump, mellowing through the seasons and returning to the nurturing earth. From the pontoon I'd seen a bulwark of uniform gray, but here were earthen tones, a patchwork of orange-tan, and gold, and ash-blue, assembled by master quilters rather than stoneworkers. A riot of flora swarmed at its edges, poised to overrun it, an oncoming and benevolent tide from the shore, a deluge of amorphous greens and pale yellows and hints of violet. Even in the fitful gleams of the flashlights, the water lazed by with regal disinterest, sleepy in its storybook blue, brushstrokes of a master at child's play.

A moth settled and stuck in the paint. We needed to get that painting indoors. The sound of a splash recalled the artist himself to mind. We walked to the water's edge. The moon had popped full from the running clouds, and the stars were coming on. And there was the pontoon, adrift and unmanned, already a good swim off the dock.

"I could have sworn I tied that on," I said. And then the pontoon swung slightly, and we could see the artist lying flat on his front, reaching over the side with some makeshift hand paddle.

"Uh-oh," I said. "It looks like he's headed back out." I called out, but the artist gave no response. "He's being a little difficult tonight. I'll swim out and see what he's up to. If you and the boys can get the painting inside and keep an eye on Blake I'll be up in a minute. Koby knows how to hold it. I'm sorry about this."

I pulled off my shirt and shoes, waded in, then dove. It was a quick swim to the pontoon, and in a minute I was aboard. The artist was still paddling.

"Willem, what are you doing?" It was my phrase of the week.

He was still mute, but I resolved to wait him out.

Silence.

"I mean to paint again. The moon is nearly full and the stars are coming."

"I'm sure Karl will let us use the pontoon again in the morning."

"I mean to paint at night."

"Paint at night? How will you see?"

He didn't answer, but then, perhaps, he already had.

"Look, we can't take the pontoon at night without Karl's permission. Let's get where you want to be and drop anchor, then I'll go back and ask him. I think this boat has pretty good lights, if that helps."

I swam to shore and jogged to the Parenteaus. Betty and the boys were all gathered around the painting. Karl couldn't have been nicer. I promised to have the pontoon back first thing in the morning. But on the way out Betty pulled me aside.

"Jason, I know you trust this Willem person, and we're giving you the benefit of the doubt on that. But I don't think any of us knows exactly who he is, or what he might do at any given time. I'm not that comfortable with him out alone at night on our pontoon. We're going to let that go, but I'm going to insist from here on that our boys aren't left alone with him. Can I have your promise on that?"

As I jogged back to the lake, I wondered just what the hell I was doing, why exactly I'd put myself in such a position for a crazy wandering artist. But then again, with what I'd been planning for that GTO for some days now, I was as crazy as he was. Only there wasn't a trace of genius in me. Quite to the contrary. Much as I'd tried, I hadn't come up with a single strategy for answering the only important question – had Bobby been the driver? What was I going to do, ask him?

The party boat was ablaze in light, like a floating café, but deathly quiet. Its lone occupant stood at the easel, a horribly clichéd silhouette in moonlight. I hollered over that he was cleared for the night on the pontoon. I told him the painting was safely indoors. And I told him I was tossing some apples toward the boat. They splashed on three sides like bad tee shots missing an island green. I heard him crunch into one as I headed back into the woods.

Chapter 24

A NIGHT AT THE MOVIES

The artist appeared for breakfast the next day. His clothes were heavy with lake water from the swim in, but he declined my offer of a dry shirt. He sat with us on the deck, looking pale and shrunken, with eyes averted, but nibbling steadily and reaching for a third biscuit when Blake passed him the bowl. Near the end of the meal he was nodding off between bites, and then his hands began to shake. That can't be good, I thought. I grabbed a towel and draped it over his shoulders.

"You want a hot shower?"

Again he declined. At length he stood from his chair, bowed stiffly, and hobbled to his tent without comment. We wouldn't see him again before sundown.

Blake and I tidied up and headed down to dock the pontoon. We passed by the tent, which was already dead silent, and on into the wood. Coming into the pines at that time of day, when the sun had warmed only the open spaces, was like passing into some massive cooler. After the cold, the forest scents and the threat of a good soaking were the next things to hit you. Dew clung to every needle and showered down at any stray touch. It filled every fern, and swamped our ankles as we brushed by, even as we did our stealthiest Indian walks. Shafts of sharply angled light pierced through the tree cover. When we popped through we saw that a mist hung over the lake. I was relieved to make out the pontoon, floating more or less where I expected, though further out than I would have liked.

The cool of the forest was nothing to the cold of the lake. I enjoyed the morning forest, but I hated morning swims. Blake, already wise in many ways of the world, sat smugly on the dock. The shock of the dive left me to bitter contemplation. Laundry, cooking, water shuttle – what was I, his servant? How about a thank you now and then? And then I recovered my breath, got in a few strokes, and began to reconsider. Talent like his had to be a little disorienting – and probably exhausting. He may have been socially inept, or at least socially erratic, but whatever strange fever it was that drove him, it also drove an uncommon personal integrity, hard as it seemed to quite grasp it. I ticked off his contributions, the gift of the painting, the lessons for the kids, the sheetrock labor. I climbed up onto the pontoon and realized I hadn't been thinking about Bobby Bethune.

The artist had left the night's painting leaning on the rail, wrapped in cloth. I started the engine, ran in the boat, docked it, and wiped it down as best I could. I helped Blake with the quiver, and I shouldered the rucksack. By that time I'd stopped dripping, so I picked up the painting in preparation for its passage. It was an awkward thing to carry, too broad to fit under one arm. I angled my shoulders as I entered the wood, and again as I twisted through the narrow passages, protecting it with my body, wrapped though it was. Progress was slow – more than once I came around a bend to find Blake waiting for me on the path. Halfway home I took a break, and he commented that I was resting it on my feet, like a penguin with its egg. We came out of the trees like Moses & Son with the tablet from the mount, and we stashed it just inside the door.

Minutes later, another painting made its way to the Gallery. It was Jamie, coming down the driveway, with *Lakeshore From Pontoon*. His brothers served as escorts, one on each flank. The painting was uncovered, completely exposed, just as the artist had left it against the tree. Poor Jamie groped along the gravel like a reluctant tightroper, clutching the painting like fine crystal, his face grim with the charge. Kevin offered a quiet stream of instruction I couldn't quite make out. Koby, on the other hand, I could hear very well. "Keep your fingers out of the paint." And, "Watch where you're going, dumbass."

When we'd transferred *Lakeshore* to an easel, Jamie fell onto the couch, groaning theatrically with his head in his hands. The rest of us gathered around to assess the night's damage. Stuck on the surface were two good-sized moths and half a dozen mosquitoes, one of which, incredibly, was still moving. As we held our collective breath I steadied my right hand with my left, and I plucked them out, one by one. Some came out whole, their legs dabbed in blues and greens. But small bits of others remain to this day, in the texture of the stone, in the riot of the flora, in the slightest undulation of the lakewater.

Lakeshore's arrival sparked some big changes in the Gallery. First we moved Blake's bed, which I'd hoped to do the day before. In a performance to rival the Three Stooges, the three Parenteaus backed up the stairs, stumbling and yapping and whacking each other while I held up the bottom for what seemed an eternity. Then we set to the real work of rearranging the Gallery. Even without the bed, it was absurd having five people in that room, and I spent most of the session trying to keep the easels upright. We had many more opinions than we needed, Blake as outspoken as anyone. After much debate and some trial and error, *Lakeshore* went where the bed had been. The night painting stayed under wraps near the door, but we set a place for it next to *Lakeshore*. The two *Pondscapes* were together on the feature wall. The *Pines* stayed on the mantel. *Apple Trees* were grouped on easels along the south wall. *Cat* and *Garden at Noon* held down both corners, *Cat* set high over the reading chair. I shoved the TV back as far as it would go and stood *Beaver on Napkin* in front of it. Both end tables went to the basement. We spaced everything out as best we could, the rest of the furniture shifting as needed. It was still an insanely cramped exhibit, but the paintings were logically grouped. And, if they weren't exactly breathing, they weren't suffocating either. The Gallery was navigable, if not quite habitable.

When the boys had gone home Blake brought up his books. I made the bed. We sorted and stacked his clothes. By noon he had a real room, with a bed and a fully stocked bookshelf and dresser. The cat came up to inspect the new quarters, circling and settling on the dinosaur quilt just as she'd always done. It was a big moment, and I wished then that we'd waited for the artist. But he didn't emerge from his day sleep until many hours later, when Blake was settling down for the night. We heard him come in through the screen door, presumably to use the bathroom. I called down that he should help himself to the dinner I'd left for him, and I reached for the *Big Book of Illustrated Dinosaur Adventures*.

"Shouldn't Mister Willem see the room?" Blake asked.

"OK, go get him."

Blake slid out of bed and bee-lined down the stairs. I heard the two of them conversing in the Gallery. Blake was describing all the changes we'd made in the exhibit, and, by the time I got down there, was leading him on a formal tour.

"Blake, it's time for your story."

"Can't we read it in here?"

"You've got a brand new room upstairs."

"But just for tonight?"

And so, for all the effort we'd made to set up the new room, we found ourselves back downstairs, back on the reading chair. I flipped to the story Blake liked best. The artist ate quietly on the couch. I started in.

A likable herd of boneheads — a few pachycephalosaurus adults and a handful of their young — grazed peacefully on a savannah. The prehistoric sun warmed their bodies as only the prehistoric sun can do. Food was plentiful, by the looks of it, even outrageously so. Six-foot grasses ranged as far as the eye could see, and a smattering of prehistoric plants sprouted leaves as large as tables. One of the young ones worked some innocent mischief. His gigantic mother delivered a mild and loving rebuke, then nudged him to the best section of leaves. A great pteradactyl soared and called overhead. Suddenly, one of the other adults sounded an alert. A tyrannosaurus had appeared in the distance. The young dinosaurs began to panic, but were quickly steered into position by the adults, who formed a defensive ring around them.

I could see the artist go a little stiff at this juncture. He sat a little more upright and suspended his chewing. Blake chomped calmly at his apple quarters, a veteran of these cretaceous confrontations.

The behemoth carnivore drew near. His thighs bristled with muscle. His huge head, full of outrageous teeth, cocked to the side. A single coldblooded eye assessed the herd. A young bonehead began to whimper, and was soothingly hushed. The herd stood firm, resolute, steadfast. Their bonehead rams were bent at the ready. The predator sniffed and circled, looking for an opening. After some long tense moments he moved on. The bonehead herd stood down.

I took Blake upstairs to bed. When I came back down I found the artist still lingering in the reappointed Gallery. He was studying *Lakeshore.* I realized that this was the first time he'd seen it in full light, and I felt out of place standing next to him as he made his first real assessment of his own work. I was about to move away when he spoke.

"In those moments when nature is so beautiful," he said, "my mind recedes like the tide, and then the paintings appear as in a dream." His voice drifted off. For once, I had no answer. I stifled a few simpleton comments, an intruder in my own house. "I rather like this one," he added.

"Me too," I said. "Very much."

"Somber greens and half tones. There is something sad in it that is healthy."

"It's quite a collection you've put together here," I said.

"I work in a dumb fury in this place. From morning til night without slackening. And the secret is probably there – work long and slowly."

I thought about that. Long yes, slowly no. "From what I've seen you crank them out pretty well."

"Crank them?"

"Yes, produce them rapidly."

Pause.

"The light is good here."

"Nine paintings in, what, two weeks? And now a tenth," I said, pointing to the covered one near the door.

"Ah, yes, *Stars on the Lake*. We'll wait for Master Blake to unwrap it in the morning," he said. "I think it will most appeal him." I felt all the worse for moving Blake without him.

He settled onto the couch, and with that I realized how drastically Blake's move had altered the cabin's evening dynamic. With no sleeping child, the sitting room, though flush with easels, was now available after dark. And with the artist out of his early-to-bed routine, I was facing the possibility of a long sit with him. Even after two weeks I felt some uneasiness at the prospect – he was a man of many moods, and not your everyday conversationalist.

"You seem to be feeling better after the day's sleep," I said.

"Yes." Pause. "It was kind of you to arrange the boat."

"Well worth the effort. At least one great painting came out of it, and I'm sure the night painting will be great too."

"Betty regards me as an unpleasant person. So it was kind of them as well."

I had to think about that for a moment. "I'd be more concerned with what her children think. They think you're great."

At that he lit his pipe, staring at the woodburning stove as if contemplating the onset of winter. It was suddenly as if no one else were in the room. He was eerily comfortable with long periods of silence, and over his two weeks with us I'd become more comfortable not breaking them. After some time he got up and started flipping through the sparse movie collection I had on the shelf. *Jungle Book* was by far the most watched video in our household, and most of the few movies we owned were of that ilk. But there were a few targeted to grownups.

"Do you want to watch a movie, Willem? Pick one out if you'd like."

He looked at me in some confusion, contemplated for a moment, then handed me *The Bourne Identity*. I moved *Beaver on Napkin* to one side and slid the TV back into position. He watched me closely when I popped the movie in, as if he'd never seen such a thing. I brought us each a beer and started it up. From the opening scene – the rainy night on the sea, the motionless body bobbing in the wetsuit, the fishing boat – the artist began to fiddle like a child, slouching way down on the couch until his hips were over the edge. During the car chase – the pitiful red mini barreling down the tiny alley ("So...we got a bump coming up."), the nauseating wrong-way run on the Parisian highway – he rolled right onto the floor. When the chase was over ("We can never come back to this car.") he sat back on the couch, bouncing his leg like a boy needing to pee. I asked if he needed a break, and he looked at me like I was speaking in Mandarin. From that point on, every bit of cinematic action seemed to hit him like a stun gun. There were a few times when he fairly shouted. About halfway through, I got us each a second beer.

He spent the last forty minutes on the edge of the couch cushion, his back perfectly straight, sipping occasionally from his can. He watched all through the credits and stared at the screen long after it had gone blank. "Help yourself to another beer if you like," I said, "but I'm going to turn in." I rinsed our empties and headed up. Ten minutes into my Bobby Bethune ruminations I could hear the movie starting up again downstairs. The all-wood house was not much for dampening sound. He must have figured out how to work it – that was my last thought until I woke up after 3:00 and heard the movie still running. I figured he'd fallen asleep on the couch, and I went downstairs to shut it off. But he was wide awake. There were three more empties on the table. He gave me a quick look and turned back to the screen without a word. I plodded back up the stairs. It must have been his third or fourth time through the movie. I heard him head out to his tent at 4:20. This may be a problem, I thought, contemplating his blaring movies in multiple showings, night after night. But as far as I know, that's the only movie he ever watched.

Chapter 25

THE BLUEBERRY FARM

He'd been awake three nights in a row – up on the scaffolding, out on the pontoon, and in for the movie quadruple feature – but once again he was up in time to join us for breakfast. We spent the meal on the bench, sitting three abreast, Blake in the middle slurping cereal, and the artist to his left, pounding three quick cups of coffee. After the meal, with Blake and I looking on, he untied the cloth wrapping over *Stars on the Lake* and placed it on the easel we'd set for it.

This painting was bound to be different, if just on the basis of being done at night. But the difference was not at all what I expected. Black and deep blues covered most of the canvas, but they belied its general outlook. The dark had awakened something else within him, had tilted his needle even further from the seen to the envisioned, from the perceived to the yearned for. He'd faced to the northeast, and a flamboyant moon had jitterbugged in from stage right, commanding the spotlight in radiant yellows and oranges and hints of green. A childish outline of a crescent lurked within its sphere – he might as well have added a smile and a winking face, I thought. The sky to its left was a curtain of fancy, with eleven impish stars, not cold and stellar, but shaking free of their pinheaded forms and spilling over with irreverent smudges of the unlikeliest greens, like buds of new life. Each of those impertinent orbs cast a shimmering pathway on the lake, invitations to new and promising worlds. A cottony mist swirled in from stage left to fill any gaps in the night sky, a spirit from the lamp of some great genie, drawn to refute the emptiness of dark and space and death. The dark shapes of pines slept like paper silhouettes at lake's edge, props in a fairy tale drama. I stood close enough that nothing could spill over the edges, so I was awash in the starry realm, a realm of benevolent prospect. The artist had anticipated its appeal to Blake, but it occurred to me that the more "adult" you were, the more life had beaten you down, the more this painting might pull you in.

"Hey, Dad, we can't see," said Blake. I apologized and shifted over, and then no one said anything for a time. The artist shuffled uncomfortably.

"It's like a bedtime story," I said at last.

"The last page of the best one ever!"

It was one of those comments so exactly on the mark that it could only have come from a child, and it stung the artist in the best possible way. He recoiled in a flush of happiness he was just not equipped to handle, and he followed with an awkward move to the door.

"Mister Willem, do you want to go with us to the blueberry farm?"

The artist looked back without answering.

"I'm sure he needs some sleep, Blake. He was up very late."

I explained to the artist: "It's a farm where we can pick blueberries. You're more than welcome to join us."

We waited for a moment. He stared at us with an expression I couldn't quite decipher, stepped outside, and shut the screen door behind him. Then he turned and answered through the screen.

"Please some rest for the morning, and I could join at lunch and for the farm?"

"What do you say, Blake? Do you want to wait until after lunch so Mister Willem can join us?"

He nodded.

And so we held the trip until our sleep-deprived artist could take his rest. As promised, he surfaced in time for lunch, much improved after four or five hours. As I remember it, he was actually bouncy, almost hyperactive, like a kid on his way to the circus. When we fastened our belts I made him agree to stay buckled in, and to keep his head in the truck. He accepted these rules strictly at face value, with no admission or apparent recognition that he'd violated them before. While I pondered that, he dug into his pocket and handed me a quarter.

"It's not much, but it should get you to Switzerland."

"What?"

"You need money. I need a ride. It's that simple."

"Willem, are you quoting me lines from Bourne?"

"You're asking me a direct question? I thought you were never going to do that."

I had to laugh. I even knew the right response: "You never made a mistake before."

And now the artist laughed. In all our days together, it was the first time I'd ever seen him do that. Even as he convulsed, his eyes cast about like he didn't know where he was supposed to look. Blake laughed right with him, though he had no idea what we were talking about. When we'd settled, the artist dropped into a sudden state of exhaustion. He sighed and pressed his forehead to the window, and I figured we'd lost him for the rest of the ride. But just past the lake, he turned back and said:

"You take care of this car?" Pause. "It felt a little splashy on the way over here."

We all laughed again. He was very much pleased with himself. And he wasn't finished. Just after we'd taken our left at the tee he reached back in his pocket. This time he handed me an apple. I knew exactly what line was coming:

"For twenty thousand I like to throw in breakfast."

"Who pays twenty thousand dollars for a ride to Paris?"

My line was out of sequence, but the artist was clearly delighted. He laughed out loud for five or ten seconds, an odd-sounding series of convulsions, still chuckling to himself as his attention turned to the scenery. He rolled down the window, and I wondered if he'd forego his pledge and stick his head out. But he rallied once again.

"Listen to me. I've been speed talking for about sixty kilometers now."

I laughed, but couldn't think of any response. He turned back to the window. He put his elbow on the door, rotating his hand into the breeze, altering the airflow with the angle of his hand. At the final turn, we cut up the long narrow driveway, a canyon carved through the pines and winding uphill. It opened into a large clearing – a grassy lot for twenty or thirty cars in front, and a sea of blueberry bushes on the slight downslope behind.

This was the second of what I hoped would be many annual trips for Blake. The pick-your-own farm was open to the public only a few weeks of the year, just when the berries were perfect. We reported to the weighing station, where two women handed us buckets and affixed stickers to mark their empty weights.

"Last year this guy ate more than he put in his bucket," I said, nodding toward Blake. "Should we throw him on the scale? We can weigh him again on the way out." The ladies got a kick out of that and sent us out into the field.

We were free to roam to any bush on the plot. The parts nearest the entry had been pretty well picked over, so we wandered about two-thirds of the way down, near the eastern edge, and settled in where the berries were plump and plentiful. The artist was all business, his fingers clutching and dropping in one continuous motion, rustle and plop, berries inching up the sides of his bucket. Blake's motions were just as steady, picking with the right hand, transferring to the left, and stuffing his mouth. After ten minutes the artist had a quart of berries in his bucket. I counted five in Blake's.

The large cut in the wood, and the elevated position of the farm, gave us a more expansive view of the sky than we were used to having. Clouds were on the move, headed west, indifferent to those of us foraging below. A wedge of geese passed over, abdicating early for the south. The forest edge rose dramatically at the field's sidehill edges, sunlight attaching itself warmly to the leafy east wall. Back near the lot, an engine sounded, overloud, and just like that I was back in the Bobby Bethune vortex, back into thoughts that hadn't been far from the surface since he'd first pulled into our driveway. Blake wandered down the row, and the artist followed him down. I stayed where I was, picking at a single bush. It was the sixth day since Bobby had made the stick figure comment – I'd earned my plausible deniability. I'd been over the operation so many times I had it by rote. I'd be leaving Blake alone in the house. Fifteen minutes to run over there, two for the hammer, fifteen to run back. Mission gear, leather gloves. It was as good as done. But rather than think through the next logical steps – What would come next? Would he respond in turn? – I just kept cycling through the operation. I couldn't seem to get past it. The foragers returned. Blake's bucket was filled to a respectable one-third – I figure the artist must have poured some of his berries in. We headed back to the weigh station. The ladies seemed a little worn out this time – there was none of the banter from before. They weighed us out and emptied our buckets into brown paper bags.

We walked to the lot with our hard-earned produce. I was digging for the keys when Blake called out: "Where's Mom?"

I froze. What had set him off? I would never blame him for asking that question, at any time, in any place. But he'd never done anything like this, not so suddenly, and now he was sobbing. I picked him up.

The artist took my bucket and we exchanged looks of alarm over Blake's shoulder. I don't think he'd ever seen Blake cry. Blake was pointing at the truck. And then I saw it, and I understood. His mother was missing from the window, as anyone could see. The gap between father stick figure and baby stick figure was jarring, even to the untrained eye.

Chapter 26

THE VITRUVIAN MAN

Ours was a quiet truck as it worked its way down the long unpaved stretch, away from the farm and back onto the main road. Blake had his hand in the bag of berries on his lap. He was done eating, and normally I'd have asked him to stop fingering them, but I was well beyond that frame of mind. I could barely think enough to drive the truck. Near Jerry's Country Equipment the road picked up another lane, and I saw a car swerve hard into it, closing fast in my rear view mirror. I thought of shifting to let him pass, but he was already overtaking us on the outside. It was then that I noticed it was a cherry red GTO. "He must have gotten his paint job," I thought, but before I could consider it any further he drew even and slowed abruptly to our speed. For some reason I took a moment to admire the paint. The red positively sparkled, atomized under a sheen of impenetrable gloss, a nice, custom application. It really was a beautiful car.

The seats of the two vehicles were perfectly aligned. The artist pulled back a bit, and over his shoulder I saw Bobby's leering face, not four feet from the side of the truck. Bobby was going cross-eyed and pulling both hands off the wheel to tug his ears out – it was the strangest thing I've ever seen from someone driving a car. He alternated the cross-eyes with quick glances at the artist, to see what affect he

151

was having, and then at his buddies sitting alongside and behind him. I braked, and he braked to match. I accelerated and he accelerated to match. Someone tossed a plastic cup – ice and soda splattered in, and Blake wiped some from his knee. With steady oncoming traffic this was a dangerous game at fifty miles an hour. I decided to simply stop – in the middle of the road if I had to – but with a car behind us I couldn't do anything sudden. As I began to brake, the artist popped his door open wide and knocked it hard into the new paintjob. A howl came from the GTO, and it shifted away from us. I yelled out, "Willem, shut the door!" His door was so far open that he had to lean way out just to keep his hold on the handle, which he managed to do even while swinging his hips to put both feet on the sideboard. The straw hat flew off his head – for some reason I took a quick look in the rear view mirror to watch it skitter down the road. I was down to about thirty. The artist released with his right hand, steadying the door now with his left. I yelled at him again, and there was a lot of yelling from the GTO, which was still alongside us. But things seemed to go quiet just then. Everything seemed muffled and echoed. Time slowed nearly to a stop. The artist sat sideways, frozen and tensed. I had the ridiculous notion that he was going to jump across. And then he did exactly that.

Replaying the moment, as I still do quite often, I think, strangely enough, of da Vinci's Vitruvian Man. I imagine that's how the artist might have looked from the GTO as he floated above it, gracefully splayed, for that one timeless moment. Granted, he was fully attired and lacked the flowing locks and the idealized proportions. And I must be overstating the float time, since the truck didn't sit much higher than the GTO. But what I remember with absolute certainty was the level of his commitment – this was no cringing crouching lean and drop, but an all-or-nothing fully-splayed dive, the kind you might expect from a guy wearing a parachute, leaving only the bottoms of his shoes and the ends of his shapeless pants in view – and then the sobering, inglorious sound of his thud onto the roof. There was another moment of stunned silence with the artist stretched there on top, and then everything went crazy. Blake hollered, and someone from the GTO hollered, and it took off in a wall of noise, shooting out ahead of us, careening left and then right. The artist held on for a moment, and then he shot off and tumbled wildly into the weeds on the side of the road. I was tracking him and pulling over when the GTO lurched again at the edge of my vision. To this day I don't know what happened. Bobby may have tried something crazy, a stunt driver's 180, or maybe he just freaked out, but somehow he jerked the wheel enough to make it go over. The sparkling red GTO flipped once, and again. It teetered on edge, skidding and sparking on the driver's side, dropped back on its tires, and stopped dead.

I hit my flashers and told Blake to stay put – a moot command since he was clipped in his car seat. We locked eyes for a moment, and I saw that he was completely composed. "I'll wait here," he said. His fingers were quietly working in his bag of berries. Of all that had just happened – the artist's leap, the GTO's flip – Blake's calm struck me as the strangest.

The artist lay on his back in that kind of bristly grass you find only on the side of a frequently salted road. His arms and legs were flung wide, and the grass stuck up all around him as if he'd settled into a giant pin art box. "Jesus, Willem! Are you OK?"

His mouth was wide open and pooling blood. He'd nearly bitten his tongue off. He turned to his side and spat what must have been a quarter cup – it pooled and then sank into the sandy roadside soil. He looked at me then and grunted what I took to be a yes. I said I'd be right back and ran up to the GTO. One of the two passengers was not moving. Someone who must have been Bobby opened the driver's side door. It was something out of a zombie movie – he looked like he'd had the left side of his face sheared off. I looked away, and there on the cracked rear windshield was a white stick figure, a female form on a bicycle. It had been applied sideways, so the bicyclist lay flat, like stick figure roadkill, sanitary, neat.

Chapter 27

PORTRAIT OF A DUCK

Blake had vacated the Gallery none too soon. The artist would spend the next several days and nights there, sprawled on the couch. His hip bothered him such that he lay almost exclusively in one position, flat on his back with one knee up and the opposite foot on the floor. His hip and his tongue were hardly his only problems – he was generally a lot more beaten up than he'd originally let on. He'd refused any medical attention on site, standing instead with an ice pack to his mouth, watching the paramedic crews load Bobby and his friends into the ambulances. The tongue had looked ghastly enough that I'd insisted we follow the last of them to the hospital. The artist hobbled from the truck to the emergency door, but when he got inside he hid the limp, and he wouldn't admit to any injuries beyond the tongue. After a long wait on account of the more seriously injured victims, the doctor washed out the wound and told us there'd be no additional treatment. As she explained it, tongue wounds don't generally take stitches, but tend to heal quickly if the parts come together at rest – which they seemed to in this case.

Betty called from the station a couple hours later. She'd not only heard about the accident, but had read the initial report and witness statements. She said we could expect a visit from Lieutenant Samford in the next couple days. And she had updates from the hospital. One of Bobby's friends, the one who hadn't been moving, had a concussion and a non-displaced fracture in his neck. He'd wear a brace for quite some time, but was expected to recover fully. The passenger in the back seat had separated his shoulder and was generally banged up, but was expected to be out of the hospital within a day or two. Bobby himself had suffered the heinous facial injuries I'd seen first hand, and head trauma severe enough to make the treating team wonder how he'd walked away from the car. He was looking at several rounds of plastic surgery and some measure of disfigurement for life. His left ear was completely severed. It had been recovered on site, but was too badly mangled to be reattached.

Lieutenant Samford knocked on the screen door the very next morning, just after breakfast. In a tone that was officially civil, nothing more and nothing less, he asked to speak to the man known as Willem. I escorted him through the Gallery to the couch where the artist lay. With his tongue the size of a sausage, the artist could not speak. Lieutenant Samford seemed skeptical about that, but I had the emergency room report to corroborate the injury. Paperwork of any sort seemed to make him comfortable. He asked the artist to answer some questions in writing, but the artist shook his head and gestured that his hand was too sore to hold a pen. The officer seemed greatly unimpressed and turned his attentions to me.

He and I had never quite warmed to each other in the aftermath of the first accident. Perhaps I'd been less deferential than he'd liked, slightly critical, even, with his approach, which seemed to make the case as much about him as about Annie or the driver. And if we hadn't gelled then, when I was theoretically a victim, our prospects were not good now, with my role changed for the worse. As a point of fact, I was "harboring a person of interest to the department," and doing so under "conditions that were highly unusual". We sat at the kitchen table as he took my statement. I told him exactly what had happened at the accident scene, and during the earlier encounter with Bobby Bethune on the porch, altering nothing, withholding nothing. The discussion then returned to our resident artist.

"With all due respect, it seems implausible that you've had this man in your house for two weeks without knowing his last name." The officious tone was all too familiar from the first time around.

"For the record, he's been camping on my land, and storing his paintings in my house. I assume his last name begins with a 'G', since he signs his paintings that way. But I've never actually asked him."

"He seems to be convalescing on your couch. Are you inclined to ask him now? You have a child here. Don't you think you should have some basic information on a man staying in your house?"

"Given that he can't talk or write, I don't think I'd learn any more than you have."

"Sir, three people have been very seriously injured in an incident which, by your own admission, involves this man's leaping from your vehicle onto the roof of their vehicle. That's at the very least – we haven't established whether or not he actually jerked the wheel and caused the rollover directly. There's no warrant at this time, but without a last name we may have to take some precautions against flight."

"The driver of that car initiated a very dangerous situation. I'm pretty sure you have at least one witness to that effect. And this man, who you can see was also injured, was off that car well before it flipped. I believe the witness confirmed that as well." I let that settle for a bit. "But I can understand that you need the names of everyone involved."

I looked at the artist, and we seemed to come to some kind of understanding. I went upstairs and grabbed one of Blake's old alphabet books. Pointing to one letter at a time, the artist spelled out his name. G-O-F-F.

"Thank you. That is very helpful." He seemed genuinely pleased. "We would like to have a conversation with Mr. Goff as soon as he is able."

The artist may have exaggerated the pain in his hand, but the fact is he really couldn't speak for the better part of a week. They'd sent him home with some pain medicine, but after a round or two he'd quit taking it. Sucking on ice chips seemed the best medicine, and I kept a bowl in a cooler for him near the couch. Three times a day I'd head down to the basement with a kitchen towel wrapped around a load of fresh cubes, and beat them into chips on the cement floor. I moved two Adirondack chairs into the Gallery for Blake and me. Along with the easels, they made for an absurdly crowded room. But the artist seemed happy enough that we were taking our meals there with him, though he himself ate nothing but blueberries, picking them out of a toy plastic bucket for days on end. When he did move on to food that was more solid, every meal would set off a new round of bleeding. He'd spit that into a mug, which he or I would empty in the bathroom, depending on his energy levels. He dozed off a lot, and slept solidly after lunch – his nap schedule was oddly synchronized with Blake's.

His paintings were all around us, and during those meals Blake and I would comment on certain things we particularly liked in them. The artist would nod in contemplation, and occasionally even in agreement. But he seemed more interested in Blake's work than his own, urging him to his little easel after their afternoon naps. Late in the week Blake produced a memorable portrait of a duck, set on a large tablet of white drawing paper. It stood upright, its skinny yellow legs stretched to comically large feet, giving the impression of a sort of mallard clown. On the whole, it faced away from the viewer, and one purple wing, with great feathery fingers, was pulled around as if to scratch its backside. At some point, Blake must have decided that the head was too small, because he drew another, larger head around it. This second head brought things to scale, and jibed with the rest of the body, facing away, blank but for the receding beak. But the head inside the head – that was the expressive one. It was the mortified mallard, the duck inside the duck, peering out of itself in secret shame at its undignified scratching, scanning for anyone who might happen to see. It was juvenile cubism, and a window to the universal chagrin. The artist made wordless expressions – I believe they were more or less along those lines – and with grandiose gestures he insisted that the duck become a part of the Gallery's permanent exhibit.

Near the end of the week he was spitting less blood and walking around a little easier. Every couple of days he dragged himself upstairs for a shower. He was anxious to get outdoors, so the boys and I carried the couch onto the porch – me on one end and three Parenteaus on the other, with Blake holding the door – and he set up quarters there under the roof, days on the couch and nights on the daybed. He began to smoke the occasional pipe, and within a day or two he began to sketch again. It was still hard for him to stand, so he sat at Blake's little easel. He worked at various points on the deck, and later he ventured back into the yard. But he never painted in that condition. He worked only in pencil, filling one entire sketchbook and then another, hording the images as if to paint them another time when he was whole again, or perhaps in the winter when the land and skies had gone pale.

Beyond the time they helped me with the couch, the boys stopped in only once or twice, certainly less than they normally did. Maybe they felt that the artist needed quiet, but that wasn't really their style. It seemed more likely that Betty was restricting their visits. But would that have been out of respect for the recovering patient, or out of distaste for the person of interest? School was opening soon, and perhaps that had something to do with it. Betty stopped by herself one afternoon to give me a medical update. Bobby, apparently, had not regained his normal cognitive function. I wondered to myself what they were using for a baseline. The others were coming along as expected. As for Betty, I couldn't help but think her primary intent was to get a glimpse of the artist, and to report back what she'd seen.

Lieutenant Samford called every couple of days to inquire about the artist. I reported, quite truthfully, that he was still not speaking. I owned that he could now sit up, even hobble around a little bit. I felt no obligation to mention that he could also now hold a pencil and had resumed his sketching. I'd seen at least one cruiser passing by. If they were interested enough they could see it for themselves.

Chapter 28

THE CHANGING OF THE SEASONS

The first reds and yellows in the leaves are always something of a surprise. They seem early and out of place when you can still catch the scent of the sun baking your forearms, even at the very tail end of summer. But it was on just such a conflicted day that things had begun to feel normal again. The artist was back at his easel, standing and sketching. He had begun to speak again, though his diction was still well short of the mark. Blake was dragging a string along the deck, the cat giving chase, spearing at it and clutching it back. And here was Jamie, wandering down the driveway.

"Looks like Willem is getting ready to paint again," he said.

"Sketching only, but he's getting along pretty well now. How about you guys? You about ready for your next installment?"

"We have to start school on Monday," he said with a long face. "So we probably won't be painting for a while." He was picking a pine cone clean, dropping the wooden scales right onto the deck. I gave him an artist-worthy scowl to get a laugh about that, but he wasn't buying it. He was distracted, and, as it turned out, with good reason. "I'm probably not supposed to tell you this," he said after a few minutes, "but my mother says they're going to pick Willem up in the next couple of days. I guess they're just waiting for some paperwork."

"She told you that?"

"Well, no, she told my dad. But I heard her say it."

"Oh. Well, thanks for letting me know."

And that was our tipoff, straight from our ten-year-old source. What a sweet kid. I put a call in to Clare. She did some asking around and called me back just after dinner. In all likelihood, she said, they'd take him in, charge him with reckless endangerment or something of the sort, and release him on a moderate bail, or even on personal recognizance. She offered a couple names of defense attorneys out our way, although she expected that a public defender would be more practical.

The artist and I "discussed" the situation that night, or, rather I told him everything I'd learned, and he mouthed thick responses, some more intelligible than others. We were sitting in the Adirondacks, and he seemed just as interested to watch the fireflies flashing in the dark. We took the time to spar over what it was that made them flare. He was in no shape to advance any theories of his own, but was happy enough to debunk my long-winded explanation – and we both got a little laugh out of that. Back on topic, I said I'd cover his bail, if it came to that. He seemed to appreciate the offer, and overall I was impressed with how unruffled he seemed over the whole affair. But from what I could tell later that night, he didn't do much sleeping. I heard him shuffling around in the Gallery sometime after two, and again just before dawn.

The deck was empty when Blake and I came down the next morning. I was happy to see that the artist felt well enough to resume his early walks. Blake and I kept our watch on the road all through breakfast while I refrained from commenting on his spectacular pompadour. A doe showed itself in the clearing, and a red-winged blackbird settled for a moment on the deck rail. But the artist did not appear. It was only when I stood to clear our plates that I noticed his bundles were gone – no trace of the tent, the rucksack, or the quiver at their familiar stoop near the door. I considered this for a long minute.

"I think Mister Willem may have moved on," I said. Blake jerked up from his slouch, hyper-alert, like a forest animal listening for footsteps. We sat for another moment, and then as if by mutual agreement, we got up and went into the Gallery. There on the mantel, in place of *Pine Trees on a Summer Morning*, was the bathroom mirror. And there in the corner was a painting of the artist himself.

He was neither better looking nor worse looking on canvas than he'd been in real life. He wore an expression I remembered from one of his first mornings with us. It was a look of simple, unmasked skepticism, bordering on a very personal distrust. I'd seen that look when I'd explained to Blake that the cat had offered us the chipmunk and we'd thrown it into the woods so as not to hurt her feelings. The reflected artist was hatless – a presentation I'd rarely seen – and he appeared to have combed his hair for the sitting. He wore the familiar collarless white shirt, but a coat and vest I hadn't seen before, in greens and grays, with purples in the folds. I guessed that he'd painted them from memory, or entirely from his imagination. His beard was true orange, but his face, the part of it in shadow, ran to the strangest tone – lizard green is the only way I can describe it. Swirls from the colors of his jacket filled the canvas around him, like smoke lifting from some great psychedelic fire that engulfed him.

An empty envelope leaned against the canvas. Inside was a single sheet, twice folded, with a single inscription. I read it aloud:

"One may have a blazing hearth in one's soul, and yet there is a sadness if no one comes to sit by it. It is good work I have done here. I shake your hand in thought. WG"

"Do you think he's coming back?" Blake asked.

"I was just wondering that myself," I said.

But he was gone, as strangely as he'd arrived. The accident and its aftermath had almost certainly pushed him out, but it was never going to be forever. And in the end, the quiet exit was probably the best path.

It made an honest man of me when Lieutenant Samford and another officer stopped by the next afternoon. He'd left without our knowing, I said, and I didn't know where he'd gone.

It certainly wasn't my place to go looking for him. I'd offered to hold his work, and I figured I'd do exactly that, for as long as it took him to come back for it – even, I guess, if that was never. And then *Pine Trees on a Summer Morning* came back to mind, and I knew. I flipped the self portrait – and there it was, on the back side, rudely inverted. I knew for a fact he had plenty of canvas, the bastard. I had to laugh.

That autumn was the most spectacular I can remember. The big maple turned a yellow so bright that some days I could hardly bear to look directly. The reds and oranges were like the banners of some great coronation. I couldn't help but think what the artist might have done in that riot of foliage. I hoped the colors were as rich wherever he was.

Chapter 29

AN EARTHY SLEEP

Betty had broken bad news before. And on a chilly night in early November, when the colors of autumn were lost and lamented, our faithful neighbor and trusted dispatcher was at it again. Through what she called the national watch, the Pinewoods Police Department had been notified of the death of Willem Goff, person of interest. The body had been found near the border of Maine and New Brunswick. Cause of death: exposure.

I stayed up all that night in the Gallery, gazing at paintings and jotting down whatever came to mind. The artist had left us just a few months earlier – the memories were fresh, visceral, a bite of a sandwich, a jot of an eyebrow. Every moment I recorded felt like a single brushstroke on many canvases, a tiny piece of the history of every painting in that room.

Had he taken up with anyone, caught any rides, found any places to stay? Or had he just walked north, straight into the cold, for weeks and months on end? I'd pictured him painting madly through that autumn of outrageous foliage. Ideally he'd have chased it south, but maybe he'd just lost his head in that canopy of color. I imagined his supplies running low. I imagined him going to the flip side of his canvases. I imagined him working until the end, and I tried not to think beyond that – the paint going stiff on the brush, his hands trembling and cracking in the cold, the onset of darkness and the miserable frigid night, the body in retreat, death from the edges. I hoped he'd crawled into his earthy bag, in his earthy tent, and slept the most beautiful unending earthy sleep.

In the morning Betty got me the name of the town. I didn't know if the artist had kept up with anyone, or if I could expect any next of kin – a parent, a sibling, an ex-wife – to appear and claim the body. A Sergeant Milansky told me that nothing on the victim's person had indicated as much, and he proceeded to grill me on the point. My calling to ask after a man of whom I knew so little struck him as suspicious, as if I were some kind of body-snatcher working leads for deceased and unclaimed drifters. I was more direct with the man at the morgue: "Listen, I don't know that much about the guy – he was pretty quiet. But he was a friend of mine, and if nobody else claims him I'll come up and take care of things."

Blake and I were on the road before noon. I planned on seven or eight hours of driving, with some pretty miserable roads along the way. I still didn't know if anyone would show up in the end to trump me – I'd have been happy enough if they had. Blake had his first overnight in a lousy motel. We had a big trucker's breakfast. And when we pulled into the morgue, we were the only takers. We filled out the paperwork, made the arrangements, did what we needed to do. There wasn't much for personal effects. He'd been found in his tent. The rucksack was missing. And the quiver was empty. Had he crumpled his sketches for fire-starters, snapped his stretchers and easel for teepees and cabins? We took the hat and the pipe, the quiver and the shoes.

I explained to Blake the concept of spreading ashes, and on the long ride home we had plenty of time to debate our options. We thought of the places where he'd stood to paint, but there was no art in pouring ashes off the edge of the deck or on the side of the road. We considered paddling out and pouring them in the beaver pond, but it still seemed a little too close to the road. We thought of paddling out into the lake, but recalling his inglorious swim at the dock, we thought otherwise. In the end, we spread his ashes in the Dominion of the Pines. It was the most peaceful place we could think of, and we knew he'd loved it as much as we did.

The first real snow of the season set in the day we did it. The green of the lawn was going pale and muted as we left the first tracks of winter and passed into the woods. There the early snow was mostly trapped overhead. As we reached the Dominion, the floor of needles was just beginning to moisten. I poured half the ashes, and Blake poured the other, and big flakes began to break through the tree cover, a few of them settling in his lashes. We stood there in the deathly quiet, snow dropping all around us, until the artist was properly covered in a shroud of perfect white.

"Like a blank canvas," I said. I reached for his hand, and we headed back to the woodstove.

Blake set the artist's shoes near the front door, on the deck planks, where he'd been used to seeing them. From then on, even in the cold, he'd stop, untie his laces, and set his own shoes alongside them before going in. For my part, I pulled the drafting desk from the basement, set it in the Gallery, and sat there four or five hours a night, surrounded by the eleven paintings and the napkin, setting down as many particulars of the artist's visit as I could remember. I swiveled every couple hours to cycle through the full set of paintings, but for the most part I sat still, scribbling there for the better part of two months, until, to my great surprise, I found that I'd finished. I printed one copy, and in the course of a week's bedtime, just before Christmas, I read the best parts to Blake.

Blake found his first pair of skates under the tree a few days later. Conditions were perfect, and I put him on the ice for the first time on Christmas afternoon. He was a natural skater from the first go, and after a time he seemed to sense that, to understand that he was a creature perfectly designed for the purpose. Cold as it was, he couldn't get enough of that perfect little pond. We were out there every day after breakfast, and then again after lunch, sometimes free skating, sometimes with a stick and puck. One afternoon I tied a string of balloons to his shoulder – they flew behind him like a tightly leashed kite. Blake kept skating, long after they'd shriveled in the cold.

Toward the end of the week I pulled Annie's camera from the closet. It was the first light that camera had seen in years. The single picture I took that day is the earliest I have of Blake as a real boy, the first since he'd been a baby. It's a family icon now, framed and settled on the bookshelf, five-year-old Blake in his skating gear on the frozen beaver pond. He's thickly bundled in a thick winter hat with earflaps, a blue jacket, black snowpants and red mittens. An instinctive hockey sense shows through all the layers. He holds the stick with his hands spread just right, his feet spread just right, and the blade flat on the ice. His knees are bent slightly over his inside edges, just like they should be. His head is up. He's smiling like a swashbuckling pro.

He stood only a moment for that shot, and then he was gone, zipping around the pond, and veering off the main open body onto paths of ice that wound through the wheat-colored patches of winter reeds. He'd pass in and out of view, his hat and earflaps just visible where the reeds were thin. And then there'd be a clearing, and I'd see him in full stride, stick out front, skipping neatly over any bits of icebound branches that jutted up, small hazards on an almost perfect surface.

AFTERWORD

It's been eleven years since I wrote *The Artist in the Pines*. Once I'd read the best parts to Blake, I shoved it in the drawer, next to the quiver, hat, and pipe, and I didn't touch it for a decade. The paintings stayed just where they were too, through all the years that followed. Blake's duck was perched among them, just as the artist had instructed.

The fall after the artist's death, I went back to teaching, and Blake started in at school. Just about then, he started wearing his shoes in the house again. Whether he'd forgotten or consciously decided, I don't know. I didn't ask. But we left the artist's shoes right where they were, on the deck, cracked and sunken, and we walked by them all through the seasons, year after year.

Blake and I stumbled across a nice frame at an antique store one weekend the following summer. It was ornate and wooden, and I bought it on a hunch. It turned out to be just about right for *Pine Trees Before the Dusk*. I'd read that oil paintings like to breathe and do best without glass, which made things easy, and I framed it up without too much trouble. It looked great, and with that one under our belt we got more serious about finding more frames, nice old wooden ones worthy of the artist's work. Sometimes we'd find a frame on its own, but usually we'd have to buy someone's mediocre painting and pull it out. We must have covered every shop in a fifty-mile radius. We were very picky – Blake even more so than I – but after a few years we'd managed to frame them all, including the two-sided canvas. I found an old mirror stand and rigged it up with identical frames clamped back-to-back over the single canvas. For a time we had it in the middle of the room for the double display effect, but after a while it drifted to a wall. We'd rotate it – *Pine Trees on a Summer Morning* to *Self Portrait* and back again – just like you'd flip your calendar, on the first of every month.

The hullabaloo very nearly passed us by – it was well underway before we'd even caught a sniff of it. I was leafing through one of the magazines in the school library and came across an exhibition review – in Toronto, the work of the late Willem Goff. I had to be the most excited guy on earth to read about an exhibit that had closed some thirteen months earlier. I scrambled for more news on Willem Goff in any art publication I could find. And there was plenty to be found. For a guy lying out there in the woods, he'd really moved up in the world. Our artist in the pines was already a minor celebrity. A string of quiet transactions, a handful of private collections pieced together, a run on prices, a few exhibits with the accompanying quite favorable reviews – in a few short years he was beyond anything I think he'd ever imagined for himself. The former person of interest to the Pinewoods Police Department had become an ongoing person of interest to the greater world of art.

Blake and I went to every show we could over the next few years – two in New York, one in Montreal, one in Boston. I was thrilled to see him get his due. And it was fantastic to see all that he'd done, though we both loved our paintings best. Blake told one of the security guards about our collection, but the man didn't take much of an interest. After that, as far as I know, Blake didn't bother telling anyone else.

Earlier works had surfaced from Europe, in a darker, slightly less beloved style – I wouldn't have even recognized them as his. But the bulk of his work, and by far the most accomplished of it, had come from the most obscure parts of Canada and northern New England, from roadside restaurants, boutiques, pawnshops, farmhouses, attics, and barns. The trail of discovered paintings left a geographical framework of his life, particularly from the latter years. But his personal history remained largely in shadow, despite the efforts of more than a few biographers to uncover it. A few of them called the cabin, tracking me, I suppose, from the morgue records. I never picked up.

It was a thrill to contemplate our own collection in view of all the acclaim. And it was nice to be validated in my early amateur's appraisal of his work. But I didn't expect the swell of enthusiasm to impact us one way or the other. His paintings were selling routinely at six-figure prices, but I was never going to sell anything he'd left us. Although, admittedly, it was a hell of a safety net. To tell you the truth, I'd worried more about the paintings in the early years, when I didn't think they had any particular market value. I'd lost track of the Bethunes – though I'd heard they'd sold that house too and taken an apartment a couple towns over – but I worried myself sick imagining the scarfaced Bobby Bethune and his pals breaking in to cut up the paintings. Only much later did I learn that Bobby had never quite recovered. He'd become a ward of the state.

In the wake of the accident I'd kept the memories of the artist to myself. The Parenteaus moved to Florida a couple years after Willem's death, and after that there wasn't much of anyone around who'd had any exposure to him. Pinewoods is hardly the art appreciation capital of the world – I don't know if anyone from the police department or anyone connected with the accident ever linked the person of interest to the painter of acclaim, but nobody ever mentioned anything, and I wasn't going to bring it up.

The next half a decade saw a continued trickle of newly discovered Goffs. Rather than having a dilutive effect, these served to keep the artist in the limelight, each fresh work warranting yet another public auction, or another highly publicized private gift. Institutions were tripping over themselves to build collections before it was too late. *Farmscape in Vermont* sold at auction for just over a million dollars. A few years later, *Maples by the Mill* sold for six. By almost any measure – critical reception, popular acclaim, derivative movements, market pricing – Willem Goff had become one of the most important artists in many decades. It was difficult to contemplate. I remembered how nervous the ten-year-old Jamie had been walking *Lakeshore from Pontoon* down the driveway, and I realized now just how right he'd been.

Those prices, rather than making me happy, as you might have expected, worried the hell out of me. All of Willem's work had been great, in my eyes, from the beginning. I can't tell you how many nights over those years I just sat there in the Gallery, hours on end, no book, no television – I'd gotten rid of the television entirely – just staring at those paintings. They weren't getting any better on account of their market value. Meanwhile, most of his work had already migrated to the great museums, with state of the art security systems, closed circuit television, round-the-clock staffing. And there we were, with eleven paintings and an unsigned napkin crammed into one room of our country cabin, in plain sight through the first-floor windows, in a house I never even used to lock. By the time Blake was getting ready for high school, it was starting to weigh me down.

The more I loved that collection, the more I worried about it. That was unfortunate, because I was generally worrying less about things. Blake was a happy kid, doing well, with a good group of friends. He'd never shown much curiosity about who'd driven the car that had killed his mother, and I'd never encouraged any. For my part, I'd become more settled over the years with the notion that Bobby had been the driver, and that with a nudge from the artist he'd paid his price. I still had no real evidence on the point, but it was a narrative that seemed to sit well with me, even on the off-chance it was fiction. For a while I'd toyed with the notion of working on Bobby's friends to see what they knew, but at some point I just let it go. Years of teaching, and the social interactions involved in raising a child, helped me to move along. I was feeling inclined to more social behavior, feeling more comfortable and rooted in Pinewoods. But with those paintings at those prices I found myself cringing anytime I left the cabin. I cringed even more at the prospect of anyone else coming in. Kids were fine – Blake's friends were in and out constantly. But I went to great and often awkward lengths to keep their parents at the door.

I'd never really leveled with Blake. To him, that art was just part of the furniture, the stuff he'd grown up with. He had some fuzzy memories of the artist, and some slightly less fuzzy memories of our museum trips. Much as I wanted to share our visitor's success, the last thing Blake and his friends needed to know was that his likable little duck sat in a backdrop worth sixty million.

At some point he came of age, and I came of age. I told him that the collection was too valuable to keep in the cabin any longer. Those paintings needed to be somewhere safe, and somewhere other people could see them. I told him I'd made anonymous calls to a few museums, told them we had a dozen original Goffs, and I wanted them kept together. I wasn't interested in donating just yet, but perhaps a long-term loan could be arranged.

The rest is pretty much a matter of public record. The museum sent up their own crew to pack up the paintings and a security crew with two armored cars to transport them. That was standard procedure. What was most definitely not standard was the private exhibition I'd insisted they put on before they hauled them away. Right there in Pinewoods: eleven previously unseen paintings of Willem Goff, and one sketch on a napkin, all shown on one gorgeous summer weekend, at no charge to the public, on the very grounds where they'd been painted. The museum crew hung banners on the roof, storyboards on the walls. They put half the paintings – those of the garden, pondscape and pine trees – under bright sunscreens on the deck, where views of the latter were just as the artist had seen them. The rest they arranged in the Gallery, with special supplementary lighting. They set his personal effects – the straw hat, the pipe, the shoes and the quiver – like a sort of expanded still life, with a vase of irises on the old wooden kitchen table.

I'd tracked down the Parenteau boys and flown them in for the weekend. I hadn't seen them in years, and they'd grown up the way people do, the same and nothing the same. Jamie was nearly six-three, a full head taller than Koby. Kevin was a steady stream of one-liners. On the night before the opening I walked them back through the Gallery. And then I took them all out for dinner, and we talked about how crazy it had all been. How every piece in the whole exhibit had been painted in our little slice of the woods. How we'd all sat around and watched Willem Goff paint *Cat,* start to finish, in about forty-five minutes. How we'd interrupted *Garden at Noon with Figure* for a game of frisbee. How he'd left *Lakeshore From Pontoon* leaning on a tree, catching bugs like flypaper. How little kids with flashlights had carried that painting, completely unprotected, through the night woods. How I'd plucked the bugs off it the next day, before they'd completely dried in place. And how *Stars on the Lake –* which may already be the most celebrated discovery in the last century of painting – had been left floating on an unmanned party pontoon.

Blake had been too young to remember much, but the four of us were able to fill in some of his blanks. The accent, the pipe, all the little mannerisms. Kevin could do a passable imitation of his manner of speech, of his quick-stepping and hand-delivering the frisbee. I told the story of his falling off the pontoon, and later, when they asked, of his Bourne-like leap onto the GTO. At the end of the meal I handed one pastel cat to each of them, their own personal collaborations with the great Willem Goff.

For the next two days a line formed on our road, reminiscent of the one for Annie so many years earlier. Buses shuttled in from the high school lot, dropping visitors at the turnaround point a quarter mile down the road, just past where I'd first seen the artist pop out of the trees. Those in the queue – locals, people from the city, and some who'd come from far further – would file by the beaver pond, sharing the exact vantage point that the artist had chosen. As they neared the house, they'd catch a glimpse of the garden, much as he had seen it. And as they turned into the driveway they'd see the apple trees in the field across the knee wall, just as he had. Security kept them moving, through the deck exhibit, through the Gallery, and out the back door. I mostly hung around in the yard, watching anonymously as the visitors filed out. Most of them wore the same blank expressions they wore on the way in, the normal blank expressions people tend to wear in public. I wanted to go up to each of them and grab them by the shoulders and say, "Hey, wasn't that great?" But an exhibit's not a ballgame, or a concert. You're aware that people aren't going to stand up and cheer. On the other hand, you can't help feeling a little let down when they don't. They seemed happy enough though, milling around afterwards, walking through the yard or crossing into the Parenteaus' old field. Those I spoke to really did seem thrilled to have seen the work. The locals couldn't seem to believe it had all happened here in Pinewoods. Eventually they all circled back down the road where the buses were waiting. The last of them pulled out at sunset.

The museum people had begun crating up the paintings before the last visitor had hit the bottom step. I was interested to watch the professionals work, but when they shoved the first painting into its crate I realized it'd be like seeing my oldest friends packed into caskets. I watched them pack his hat and his shoes, and I imagined the artist giving me a good scowl for the audacity of my intrusion. So I left them to their work, and for the last time, I stepped out of the Gallery and into the moonlight.

THE AUTHOR

M. Reese Kennedy was born and raised in Omaha during its heyday as the world's largest livestock market, slaughterhouse, and meatpacking center. He is the author of two novels – *The Plague of Dreamlessness* and *The Artist in the Pines* – and lives in rural Australia.

ACKNOWLEDGEMENTS

My thanks to the people at the Van Gogh Museum, curators of a truly sacred collection. And to Elisabeth Lawrence, for the painting tutorial and the title page pine cone. Special thanks to my pre-publication readers, Champ Cudahy and Bill Scheft, for their encouragements and their thoughtful contributions. To Cal and Jack, who are ever in my thoughts and in these pages. And most of all to Louisa, my wife, my best friend, and my editor, who shares the world with me every day.